Now That I've Lost You

PAUL EDWARDS

Screaming Dreams

FIRST EDITION
- 2013 -

Published by
Screaming Dreams

113-116 Bute Street, Cardiff Bay,
Cardiff, CF10 5EQ, South Wales, UK

www.screamingdreams.com

ISBN : 978-1-906652-16-6

Thanks to Mum, Dad, Matt, Mark, Dan, Chris Castle, Dave Jones, Ian, Sandra & Brian Gray, Jon Hodges, Trevor Denyer, Graeme Hurry, John Benson, Kenneth Crist, Len Maynard, Mick Sims, Chris Pisano, James Cooper, David Price, Karonda & Dr. Jones, Chris Bartholomew, Paul Bradshaw, Greg F. Gifune, C. Allen & Sarah Reed and Nicole Gray for all your help, guidance and support with these stories.

Special thanks to Steve Upham, Dave Gatward, Mathew Killeen and Anne Stickel.

To Mandy, my wife and best friend: this is for you.

CONTENTS

INTRODUCTION

Paul Edwards is a *Black Petals* horror regular whose material I edit for Kenny Crist. A perusal of his outstanding 19-story collection, NOW THAT I'VE LOST YOU, gives ample testimony as to why his tales are preferred not only by us, but also by the likes of *Cemetery Moon, Dark Doorways, Dark Fire, Darkness Rising, Dream Zone, Escaping Elsewhere, Kimota, Midnight Street, Theatre of Decay,* and *Whispers of Wickedness*. Readers can count on literary quality in his surreal approach to the horror genre.

Writing most often about broken relationships within a horror context, Paul Edwards succeeds in putting a human face on difficult situations. Jealousy, rage, murder, and loss figure prominently. He takes us to the down-and-out areas of Wickham, Locksley, the American desert, and even Goa, India. Once there, clocks stop and normalcy evaporates. We look into—or through—the (usually green) eyes of losers who inhabit small spaces, whether graveyards, old churches, smoky pubs, tiny apartments, or their own echoing heads.

Outside, darkness dwells and the cold rain falls—or, in the case of Goa, heat blasts—setting a stage where unnatural urges wilt the soul. Holes in reality open up. Plague survivors turn on each other. Lovers rend the beloved. Loners seeking a cure for their isolation find heaven or hell within themselves. The lines between good and evil blur. The past is cast off. Bustling cities provide dead zones, while silent graveyards flourish with eerie life. Veins throb. Blood drips. Hypnotic highways lead into uncharted realms.

Witches, warlocks, and the walking dead put in appearances. The majority of the characters, however, are ordinary people faced with extraordinary situations, in which they must either rise to or fall from moments of grace. Not trying hard enough, many fail.

The whirlwind trip through the mad imagination of the inventive author is well worth the price of admission. But, let the buyer beware. No one can read Paul Edwards' work and remain unmoved by it. And, in my opinion, no one can adequately capture his unique style in just the few words offered here.

Anne M. Stickel
Co-editor of Black Petals Magazine
March 2008

Deep in earth my love is lying
And I must weep alone.
Edgar Allan Poe

We've met before, haven't we?
David Lynch, *Lost Highway* **(1997)**

NOW THAT I'VE LOST YOU

I move to the window. Darkening headstones stand out against the bruised sky like cardboard cutouts.

You're wearing brown leather boots, a silk lilac dress, dark, wrap-around sunglasses. Skeletons of trees whisper and sway around you.

As you step up to the porch, I shrink back into the shadows of the room. A red lamp paints my face, like a hallucination, on to the darkness of the pane.

"I'm going to save you, Kate," I whisper, over and over, until it becomes a mantra.

It started at a party Julian was throwing – a reunion for his university friends.

Broomstick thin and ashen faced, dripping with runic pendants and bangles, he flitted from one person to another, smoking Camels and knocking back shot glasses of whisky.

"Where did you get those from?" asked a boy in a *Bauhaus* T-shirt.

Julian drew sharply on his cigarette, then glanced up at the two ornate Samurai swords mounted on the wall. "I bought them in Osaka. Beautiful, aren't they?" A smile tugged at the corner of his mouth.

I fucking hated that smile.

In the kitchen, Kate's friend Scott was busy ransacking the fridge for beer. "Hi Mike," he said. "Great party, eh?"

"Have you seen Kate?" I asked. "Can't seem to find her anywhere."

"No. 'Fraid not," he shrugged apologetically, the glare of the strip-light accentuating his black, black eyes. "So, uh, how's things going between you and her?"

"Fine, yeah, real good."

"You're a lucky guy – Kate's an *excellent* girl. We used to share art classes Tuesdays and Thursdays. It was the three of us: me, Kate and Julian."

I glanced into the hall. Couples were pressed against the stairs, their faces masked by darkness. "Julian's a popular guy," I said.

"He's one cool fucking dude. I mean, look at this house. I would *kill* to have a place like this."

He moved to the window, rubbed the fog away with his hands. "Look out there, Mike. See the graveyard? This house used to be an old Methodist church. I mean, how fucking *cool* is that?"

Kate told me that Julian wrote his poetry out there; after sunset he'd lie on a tomb and smoke weed under the stars, jotting his visions down in a Book of Shadows.

I grabbed a beer and went searching for Kate upstairs. Along the landing huddled figures lay slumped under crimson lanterns like characters in a van Gogh nightscape. I inspected each face – Kate wasn't there.

A couple of teenagers brushed past me on their way to a bedroom. The girl was laughing, teeth glinting in the darkness. I followed them. The room was dark, bare. Rob Zombie howled from a beaten stereo. Crouched on the carpet, silent and still, a small circle of teenagers passed around a bottle wrapped in brown paper.

I twitched the curtain across the window. Moonlight illuminated Kate, sitting beneath the wings of a crumbling marble angel. She was with Julian and they were laughing and he had his arms around her and they didn't even notice me.

Two days before Christmas, we went shopping in the city centre. As we came out of a department store the bus was waiting for us, shivering by the kerb. We squeezed into the seats at the back and Kate took hold of my hand.

Blurred shadows flitted past the windows. Clouds trembled, flaking snow. "What are you thinking about?" Kate asked as I stared outside.

I turned to her. "What's going on between you and Julian, Kate?"

Her mouth opened, but for a few seconds she couldn't speak.

"What? What do you mean?"

"You've been spending a lot of time with him just lately."

She snatched her hand back. "What exactly are you getting at, Mike?"

"I saw you two together at the party. You were all over him."

She turned away, disgusted, but I couldn't see her reflection in the darkness of the pane.

Later, curled up in bed together, she relented. She shook me, to wake me, but I was awake anyway. "Mike," she said. "I haven't been entirely straight with you."

I sat up. She drew her coppery hair away from her eyes.

"I did have a relationship with Julian," she said, "but that was *way* before you. We only lasted a couple of weeks. It's a miracle our friendship survived, really. So yes, we are close, and you'll just have to accept that. But as a couple, Julian and I are over, okay?"

I felt sick and scared. Betrayed. "Why didn't you tell me about any of this before?" I asked.

"I…I didn't want you to worry about it. I love you, Mike, and as crazy as this sounds, I worry about what you *think* of me. But I don't want to have to hide *anything* from you ever again." She puffed out her cheeks. "That's why it's important for me to tell you this."

She smiled.

In the darkness, her face seemed paler than usual. Smudges of purple sat raw around her black, black eyes.

Julian popped around one evening to give Kate some of his poetry to read. I watched him from the other end of the hall, standing in the shadows of the doorway, his emaciated frame enveloped in a black leather coat. They were whispering something, but I couldn't quite hear what they were saying over the noise of the rain on the roof-tiles.

After he'd gone, Kate curled up in her armchair to read his poetry. Her face was scrunched up in concentration, her mind lost to his words.

Looking back, it wasn't the exchange of bodily fluids that bothered me; it was the interchange of thoughts and dreams that concerned me more. You see, these things open a person up...

Bind people to each other for eternity.

Twilight crept through gnarled trees.

I crouched in the gloaming, watching Kate and Julian drift through the graveyard together, her head on his shoulder, their fingers entwined. As he talked, Kate's hair licked and whipped about her face, coppery threads writhing in the air like snakes.

Leaves rustled, trees creaked. Marble angels glared at me with black, black eyes.

He gripped her hands, shuffled in close, whispered into her ear. I couldn't breathe. Then his mouth found her neck, and her eyelashes fluttered and her head lolled forward as his long dark coat enveloped them both.

I blinked tears, stared up at the sky, at dark, blood-washed trees.

I woke suddenly that night.

Kate was asleep, her coppery hair fanned out across the pillow.

As I gazed at her, I noticed how unnaturally white her face looked in the moonlight.

Her eyes snapped open. She looked disorientated, lost. "Where are you?" she whispered, hands reaching for my face.

The room went black. From behind the curtains a shadow passed across the face of the moon.

Everything was still. Then moonlight streamed through the curtains again, and I turned back to Kate. She was barely breathing.

I touched her throat, feeling for holes.

We spent last Sunday in our little rented house, trying to save us.

We sat on our sofa, listening to the rain claw at the windowpane. I tried listening beyond the rain, but I couldn't hear her breathe. She was smoking Camels, one after the other.

I wanted to ask her if she was going to see him again, whether she was going to sneak over there after work. But what was the point?

Then it hit me. *This* wasn't Kate. This *thing* sat next to me wasn't the woman I'd loved.

"Why did you tear up my stuff?" she asked, her eyes fixed on nothing in particular on the wall.

In the bedroom, the window banged loudly in the wind. Shredded pieces of poetry swirled across the floorboards.

I didn't say anything. Instead, I thought about the key I'd found in her handbag, and how I'd taken a copy of it at the local hardware store.

And so here I wait for you, Kate. So, so patiently I wait.

I never dreamed I'd hurt you. I never dreamed I'd lose you. Not in a thousand years. Not in an eternity.

But you were taken from me and violated. Now you're less than real.

You're not even human.

Click.

You let yourself in.

You call his name – once, twice; then make your way upstairs. I hold my breath. Behind me, Julian's body lies broken on the bed. His head stares up at me from across the bedroom floor.

Floorboards creak on the landing.

"I'm going to save you, Kate."

I grip the Samurai sword in my hand.

The door opens.

DEAD CITY BLUES

Static.

Behind it, the ghost of a face; a figure in rain. I hear a voice, too:

"...All for you..."

I move the aerial around, but the figure on TV flickers and jumps and vanishes and I swear under my breath as I set the aerial back down. "Almost got something," I groan.

Matilda doesn't reply. She's brushing her teeth, humming a lullaby Mum used to sing to us when we were small.

I twitch the curtains. "There's a man out in the street," I say, "lying on his side with his face turned away. I can see blood trickling out from under him, running down the road in a red rivulet."

I let the curtain flap back into place, sigh. "What shall we do with ourselves?" I ask, turning, perching myself upon the edge of the bed. From the bathroom, I can hear the steady sound of running water.

Matilda drifts out of the bathroom in her pretty white nightdress. "You forgot to turn the tap off," I say, but she ignores me; just stands there humming that stupid lullaby through gritted teeth.

"We could try going home. Maybe Mum's feeling better..." I cock my head. "You okay, Sis?"

Matilda coughs blood, and it's then I realise I'm all alone in the world.

Rising, I press my hands to my face and shriek. Losing her balance, Matilda moans and stumbles into the wall; from behind frazzled coils of hair her eyes roll horribly.

I dash out the room, charge downstairs, out the front door

and around the man lying inert in the road. I think I'm going to puke, but I swallow it down and tumble through an open gate into Locksley Cemetery.

Stillness. Silence. Headstones slice out of long yellow grass. Angels stare with hollow eyes. Flitting around open graves, I duck beneath gnarled branches and stumble out of the far gate. Then I'm in the street, facing my old school. It stands empty and tired, broken window frames lined with glass teeth, weeds poking out of the playground like tongues.

The day breathes. A discoloured Coke can rattles past me. *I'm all alone,* I think, but I can't cry, not yet.

I dig my fingernails into the palms of my hands. "Fuck you," I mutter to no one in particular. Then, louder: "*FUCK YOU!*"

My gaze flickers to the chimney stacks and shattered windows of the dead industrial estate opposite, stained with soot and groaning beneath the breeze as though about to collapse. Someone has spray painted words over the sign welcoming people into our town.

It now reads: WELCOME TO DEAD CITY.

A strip light flickers and hums like a trapped bluebottle. I'm in a deserted McDonalds, sipping Coke that tastes vaguely wrong. From the first floor I can look out across town; there's rubbish and debris everywhere. Most of the shop windows are broken, and I can see rats in the backyard of the Chinese takeaway. Opposite McDonalds is the toy shop mum used to take me and Matilda to whenever we'd been good; we'd go in and buy miniatures for the doll's house that we kept on our front room windowsill.

"Matilda's gone," I whisper, suddenly, and I stumble to my feet and into the toilet, puking into the sink as I stare into a cracked mirror at my own trembling reflection.

Sunlight scrapes away the shadows on the terrace houses along Foree Road.

I walk and walk, hands clenched, not really thinking about where I'm going. I start to believe that this isn't real, that it's all a dream, that I'll wake up in my room back in our

12

house on Sherman Drive and everything'll be normal again. But then I'm aware of the pain in my palms, and tears prickle my eyes as I gaze upon the vicious little half-moons imprinted on my flesh.

Later, a wave of tiredness hits me and I flop down in a shop doorway and close my eyes. When I open them again it's dark. A streetlamp flickers and buzzes, and there, standing in its insipid light, is a shadow.

My heart thuds and thunders. I grip the frame to the doorway and lever myself out. The moon drops into my line of vision, all maggoty and cracked above broken chimney pots.

The figure looks up, its face a thin white oval in the darkness. I take several steps back, clinging to the shadows. Then I spin and dart between two abandoned cars, wheeling out on to the empty main road. Glazed dead eyes rove, watching me pass.

A figure stumbles out of a shop doorway. I scream and flee as more of them rise from the shadows, groaning up at the bright full moon.

Pausing outside a shuttered Spar shop, I stoop to catch my breath. Behind me, silvery-blue faces peel themselves from the darkness. I charge toward the *Robins* cinema, barge through the double doors and flit up a narrow flight of stairs, past lurid posters for *28 Weeks Later* and *Hostel II*.

I stumble into the main screening room. The black cinema screen is at the far end, and before me are rows and rows of blood red seats. I hurry down the steps and squeeze into the space between the first and second rows.

The door into the main screening room bursts open, and I duck down quick.

Seconds pass. *Shit,* I think. *Oh shit, shit.* Closing my eyes, I bite down hard on my lip. I'm hardly breathing.

Moments later I open my eyes. I lift my head just as a figure looms over me, its sunken face crawling with worms, and I scream so loud that I think my lungs are going to burst. Then the head explodes, bits of brain and gristle showering my face, clothes, and hair. *"Evelyn!"*

I look up, startled. Steven: a lad from my English

Literature classes at school. Always so neat and presentable. Now his clothes are torn, and one of the lenses to his glasses is cracked. Thick hair sprouts dishevelled, greasy and wild from the top of his head, and in balled, trembling hands he clutches a shotgun.

"It's okay," he whispers, raising one of his hands in a placating gesture. "Everything's going to be okay now."

Sammy-Lee, my best friend at school, told me that Steven fancied me. I remember this as he holds out his hand. Ignoring it, I use the nearest seat to lever myself up. I run a trembling hand across my face. When I bring it away again, my palm is slick with blood.

Steven's hand drops to his side. "We need to go," he says.

"Where?" I whisper. "Where can we go?"

"There's a fire exit in the corner. It'll take us down on to the street."

A low moan comes from behind us and I wheel to see more of those things stumble slowly, gracelessly into the room. Steven barges the door open with his shoulder and then we scramble out on to the fire escape and down a set of rusting stairs into the main shopping precinct below.

The precinct is eerie and quiet; most of the streetlights are out. Windows are smashed; jagged pieces of glass sparkle in the darkness like teeth.

"Look out," Steven hisses, and I turn to see a face pour out of the shadows like milk. He pulls the trigger and the head explodes, showering us with gristle, brain and pieces of shattered skull. Gagging, I turn away.

"It's like Romero," Steven says, eyes glinting behind red-rimmed glasses. "You know, the dead films? Night, Dawn, Day?"

I stare at him.

"You got to shoot them in the head. It's like…it's like the only way to stop them."

The dead thing stumbles and lurches and falls sideways into a pile of rubbish, a piece of bloody flesh flapping where part of its head used to be. "God," Steven whispers, raking a hand through his hair, "sorry, I'm not thinking straight." He looks at me, eyes shifting nervously across my face. "This isn't the movies. *Fuck.* This is real."

Another loud moan comes from behind us.

"Come on," he urges, gripping my wrist. "There's a clothes store... I broke into it the other day. There's an exit at the back of the shop on to Cardille Road. We won't be trapped if they...come for us."

I glare at the motionless figure on the floor. "*Come* on," he urges, tugging my wrist, pulling me away.

We hurry to the large double doors of *Next* and he barges them open with the butt of his gun and then we're inside, shutting, locking, barricading the doors.

Jumping up on to the counter, Steven breathes out long, slow and hard. Watches me as I stare into the palms of my bloodstained hands. "The nights are the worst," he says, breaking the taut silence between us. "They're more active at night. Plus, you don't see them. They come out of nowhere. And if they scratch or bite you, you've had it; you become one of them."

I think of Matilda; of the stranger who had come up to her in the street and how he had taken a bite out of her. Blinking tears, I fold a blind over the window. "You'll be okay," he continues. "Stay with me, and you'll be all right." He laughs. "You didn't look twice at me at school. It's okay, no one did. Not really. It's because...well, I'm different. I didn't value the same things *they* did. Football. Brand names on clothes." His shoulders sag. "It's no wonder they didn't last five fucking minutes when it all..." His eyes narrow into slits. "You okay?"

"Sure." I come away from the window, blinds popping back into place. He jumps down from the counter. "We should think about bedding down for the night, somewhere other than here. I'm not sure we're safe..." He stops as I drift over to a radio on a windowsill. I flick the power switch; suddenly, interference fills the room.

Behind all the static, the noise, a voice:

"*...to see what I can do...see me differently...who I really am...*"

"Can you hear that?" I ask, turning, eyes widening.

Hurrying over, Steven crouches and listens carefully, hard.

"Can't hear a thing," he says after a while. "I've sat in front of that thing for hours. The TV, too. But I never pick anything up."

"I swear I heard something."

He flicks the power switch. "Ssh!"

"What?"

He nods to the window.

Things are moving out there, scratching frantically against the glass with black, blood-caked nails. "Come on," he whispers. "We'll sneak out the back."

We weave past a couple of mannequins and make our way to the exit at the back of the shop, where a frosted pane of glass splashes a cold shard of moonlight on to the walls. As we near the door, a shadow passes across the glass and Steven turns to look at me, finger pressed to his mouth. Then he crouches, lifting the letterbox. "There's one out there," he says.

He lets the flap down gently, then glances behind us. There's a fire-axe encased in glass on the wall. "Here," he says, pushing the shotgun into my hands, "we need to preserve ammo. I can take him; I know I can." Straightening, he breaks the glass with a sharp blow from his elbow and prises the axe free.

I gaze at the shotgun, smooth the shiny black barrels, the handle, fingertips flicking over the trigger.

"Get the door," Steven hisses, and I look up, nod, and then turn the handle. He kicks it open and screams as he steps out, wielding the axe around over his head. I see a stark-white face. Then the axe comes down with a *crack* and the dead thing crumples. "Got you," Steven laughs. "Got you, didn't I, you little fucker!"

He turns to me, face spattered with blood. "Let's go!"

I glare at the thing on the ground with the axe sticking out of it, and press a hand over my mouth.

For some reason I want to laugh.

We dart out of the back alley and into a large, deserted residential area. Two streetlamps hum, coating the pavement with light. Steven leads us down the side of a house and we come to some overgrown bushes. He glances behind us, to check there's no one there, then parts the foliage and slips into the darkness. I crawl through after him, bushes snapping shut behind us, briars catching in my face, hair, clothes.

Steven reaches for an apple. I peer around, noticing the small boxes of ammo, a machete, an axe, a wickedly serrated knife, chocolate bars, Ritz crackers.

A den.

"Want something?" he asks, but I shake my head. "Suit yourself."

I watch him eat. "Where did you find the gun?" I ask at last.

His gaze drops to the weapon in his lap. "It belonged to my neighbour. He showed it to me and my Dad once. Kept it in the cupboard under the stairs in one of those sports holdall thingies."

"You always used to stare at me," I say, suddenly, and Steven stops eating for a moment. Shrugs.

"Didn't think you noticed." Smiling shyly, he says, "I...like you."

I don't know what to say to that.

"Doesn't matter anyway," he mutters through a mouthful of apple. "The past's obliterated. Whatever happened before...well, it's meaningless, isn't it?"

"No," I mutter, suddenly, tears springing into my eyes, "this *can't* be real. This is... madness!"

Steven hangs his head. "I'll look after you," he says softly. "I promise I'll be here for you. We can get through this together, right? Just as long as we *trust* each other."

"I'm tired," I say.

Steven falls silent and I sit there with my eyes closed for some time. Later, when I open them again, Steven is motionless and I watch his eyelashes flutter as he dreams. I close my own eyes and when sleep comes, it's punctuated by stark, frightening images.

A figure barely discernible behind static.

Matilda smiling.

A mannequin's bland, blank stare.

Broken fingernails scratching against glass.

A marble angel.

Steven's grinning, bloodstained face.

I'll look after you.

My eyes snap open.

Dawn light filters into the den and I gaze across at Steven, asleep, his head cushioned by foliage. My eyes slide down to the shotgun in his lap. Slowly, very slowly, I reach for it. My fingers circle the barrels, grip it. Steven murmurs and mutters and I stare at him for a moment, watching, willing him still. Then he's motionless again, and I lift the gun and bring it up to my chest. I look around, spying the ammo in their little red boxes. I tip some of the cartridges out, grab them, stuff them into my jacket pocket. Then I pull back the bush and a thorn sticks into my thumb and I want to scream, to cry out, but my teeth clamp together and I crawl from the darkness as quickly and quietly as possible.

Sunlight flares over the silhouettes of houses. I glance up and down the road but there's no one around. I race toward Cooper Lane, my footfalls echoing between rows of silent terraces. The newborn sun bleeds over torn tangles of barbed wire that hang from crumbling walls, stark against the scarlet sky like rows of shattered teeth.

Cooper Lane is, like every other street in the city, eerie and quiet. I try to remember the number of his house. I glance up at a line of windows, notice scarlet curtains and dust-lined pane. That's it, I think: his room.

I perch on a bench in the park opposite, and have this crazy notion that I can see Steven's face in the apocalyptic clouds above. I blink twice, rapidly, and stare uneasily at the gun in my hands. I remember watching Steven load it; he made it look so easy. I glance around. One of those *things* is shuffling about in a shop doorway on the other side of the road. I think about shooting it, but lower the gun and walk over to the house instead.

The front garden gate hangs from a rotten hinge. The front door is locked, but the patio doors around the back aren't. I slide them open and step into the living-room.

The clock's stopped. Galaxies of dust swirl through the air. I edge around the furniture and enter the hall. To my right, a flight of stairs leads up to the first floor. I grip the railing and ascend, shotgun clenched in my hand.

The floorboards creak beneath me as I step into Steven's room. It's furnished by a single bed, a chest of drawers, a portable TV and DVD player and a lava lamp. Above the bed, sellotaped to the wall, is a poster for a movie, *Zombie*. Beneath the picture of a maggot-ridden corpse are the words: *We are going to eat you.*

Drifting over to a shelf stacked with DVDs, I run my finger along their spines.

Tombs of the Blind Dead. The Serpent and the Rainbow. Carnival of Souls. The Living Dead at the Manchester Morgue. Zombie Creeping Flesh. Dead and Buried. The Beyond. Burial Ground.

I pull open drawers. Inside, magazines: *Dark Side, Fangoria, GoreZone.*

I turn and scream. Steven's hovering in the doorway, watching me carefully, intently. "What are you doing?" he says.

"You," I hiss, pointing the gun at him. "I *knew* it. *You've* done this. *All* of this! You're *controlling* this somehow!"

He pales. *"What?"*

"I-I don't know how you did it, but make it stop. Make it stop NOW!"

He shakes his head. "I don't know what you're talking about."

"I'm trapped in your sick fantasy, aren't I? You and me; to be *alone* like this, in this…*sick* and vile world! It's like I've walked into your head; into your *fucked-up* brain!"

"Evelyn…" He takes a step toward me.

"Don't come any closer! I know what this is now. You want to look after me. Protect me. So that I…"

My hands are trembling, but I keep the gun trained on him.

"Please." He takes another step. "Give me the gun – we're not safe here. I really don't…"

And then I pull the trigger and the shot blasts through the lens covering his left eye and sprays blood and brain all over the wall behind him.

Silence.

PAUL EDWARDS

I take several steps forward, shaking, smoke billowing from both barrels of the gun.

"It's done," I whisper, softly, and laugh. A hoarse, crooked, empty laugh. "The spell...It's *broken.*"

I charge out of his room, rush down the stairs, fling open the front door...only to see the thing in the shop doorway turn its stiff, bloodstained face toward me.

I cup a hand over my mouth.

I close my eyes.

I scream and scream.

MINE

He touched the glass. Sharp pale-grey eyes held his stare.

"Dad?"

Martin stepped back quickly, away from the mirror, away from his desk and his beat-up PC.

"What are you doing?" Abigail asked, arms folded, frowning from the shadows of the stairwell.

"Working," he said.

She stared searchingly into his face. "Doesn't look like you're working."

"Stretching my legs," he replied.

She glanced into the mirror. "Dinner's ready. Are you…"

"Ten minutes," he told her. "Tell your mother I'll be ten more minutes."

He skulked downstairs three-quarters of an hour later. "Sorry," he said, shrugging meekly, pulling out his chair. "Got carried away."

"We'd almost given up on you," Belinda said as Martin took his place at the table. She twisted a strand of greying hair around her finger. "How's it going?"

He picked up his knife and fork. "Good," he nodded.

"Nearly finished?"

"Guess so."

Sighing, Abigail picked up her fork and stabbed at the small piece of haddock on her plate. "Can I go out on Friday?" she asked her father. "Jenny's…"

"No," Martin said. "We've been *through* this."

"Martin," Belinda interrupted, "she *is* sixteen. It wouldn't hurt…"

Martin kicked the table, trembling the cutlery, plates and

condiments. "You know what it's like out *there!*"

Abigail shrieked, threw down her fork and ran sobbing from the room. "Now look what you've done!" Martin spat vehemently.

Belinda glared at him in disbelief. "What *I've* done?"

Her eyes flickered to the curtained window behind him. "We should never have moved here! We should have stayed in England. I've never liked this place."

Setting her knife and fork down, she hid her face behind her hands. "She needs *friends,* Martin. She needs her independence – can't you *see* that?" Her voice softened. "This town's no good for *anybody.*"

"It's been good for me."

She dropped her hands into her lap. "Your agent was on the phone just now. He wants to know why you're not returning his calls." She stood before he could reply, and collected up the finished plates.

Martin stared into space. Then, pushing out his chair, he twitched the curtain across the windowpane. Outside, fog billowed and swirled and faces smudged into view, glaring at him.

They wanted Belinda.

They wanted Abigail.

"You can't have them," he hissed, and he took his hand away and let the curtain flap back into place.

Martin glanced at his watch. It was almost eight. He licked a finger, turned a page in his notepad and wrote, images spilling out of his head and on to the page.

A lizard-thing with three diamond-shaped eyes and a thin, forked tongue. Half-human creatures with melted faces. A short, strange-looking man with pointed ears and a malevolent grin. Devils with scabrous wings. A spider-thing with many jointed legs...

He wrote, but they were only half-realised ideas, nothing more.

He glanced at his watch, groaned, and threw his pen down in frustration. It was a quarter to ten. He needed a drink. Bad.

He ransacked his drinks cabinet but he was out of whisky.

He didn't want to go outside, but had no choice. "Won't be long," he shouted as he trudged downstairs, shrugging into his coat. "I've got my key. Remember – don't let *anybody* in."

Belinda watched him leave, then stared into the long dark shadows of the house without saying a word.

A stark red moon shone through shredded veils of fog. Shoving both hands into his pockets, Martin hurried past rows of shuttered houses.

Shapes appeared: vague forms, undeveloped figures, lurking in doorways and alleyways. At one point he glanced at a person beneath a streetlamp, and his heart skipped a beat when he saw a partially-melted face...

He reached Main Street. Lights from windows and shop doorways dripped on to the road. He passed the antique shop and Book Barn, before ducking into the grocery store.

A bell tinkled. Bill Hampton, the shopkeeper, looked up from behind the counter. The shop was quiet. Martin was the only customer here. He went straight to the liquor section, then picked up the cheapest bottle of whisky.

"Evening," smiled Bill as Martin approached the counter.

"Hi, Bill."

Bill wrapped the bottle up in tissue paper. "Anything else I can get for you?"

Martin shook his head. "No. No, thanks."

In the mirror behind the counter, Martin saw the man with the sharp pale-grey eyes smile at him from a pinched, sallow face.

"Something wrong?" Bill asked, arching an eyebrow.

"No," Martin replied quickly, blinking, shaking his head, "nothing's wrong." He passed the money over, then swiftly left the shop.

As he neared home, he glanced once – briefly, nervously – over his shoulder. Something was following him, he was *sure* of it. He scurried down the garden path, fumbling through his pockets for his key. Then, just as he unlocked the front door, a leathery face flicked a tongue at him from behind a thin curtain of fog.

He slammed the door.

"Shit."

He fought out of his coat, kicked off his shoes. Behind the door's frosted pane, a shadow pressed itself up against the glass. Clutching his whisky bottle, Martin went straight to his study, to the loft, and shut the door tightly behind him.

A solitary lamp spilled orange light on to the carpet. Belinda had her back to him, staring solemnly out of the bedroom window.

"Is Abigail in bed?" he asked.

"Yes," she replied, lifelessly.

He stood there quietly, trying to think of something else to say. He was drunk and tired; edgy. Eventually he settled on: "I'm sorry. The time just…went. Didn't realise I'd been writing for so long." He dropped his shoulders. "Please, don't be angry. Everything I do is for the best. You've heard the stories…about those *things* out there. I *worry*, love; I worry that I might lose you."

"I'm tired," she said. "I'm going to bed." As she turned away, Martin caught sight of his own reflection, grinning at him from the dark of the windowpane.

Out of the chaos, out of all the fragments, he tried to assemble meaning; to structure a narrative, a story. He'd laid down a scene, but he didn't know where to go from there.

He read and re-read the passage by the frail light of a crimson moon. It described the brutal murder of a woman and her daughter – her only child – in a house in a town buried by fog.

He stacked up his papers and drifted downstairs. Belinda was on her own in the living room, perched right on the edge of the settee, staring vacantly into space.

Martin went to the window. Outside, tendrils of white crept up the garden path. "It doesn't feel as if there *is* an outside world," Belinda said, quietly, "what with that fog and being in here all the time."

"Where's Abigail?" he said, turning to her.

"I…let her out," Belinda said, and she looked at him. "She's in town with Jenny."

Martin's jaw dropped. "What?" Grabbing his face, he glared vehemently through his fingers at her. "W-what have you *done?* Our daughter! *My* daughter! How *could* you? How *could* you do this?!"

He slammed the door just as he heard her scream after him.

He drove through New Bedlam. It was difficult to see; fog had buried the entire town. He drove around the same old streets and avenues, past partially-erased shops, houses, and garages. Eventually he discerned a group of young people gathered beneath a streetlamp, and he slowed right down. One of the group looked away as he drew up.

"Abigail!"

He flung open the door.

The group of youths shuffled away, eyes glinting nervously, suspiciously, warily. "Abigail!"

She turned to him, peeling away from the rest of the group. "What?" she said. "What is it, Dad?"

"Get in the car."

"Dad, I'm…"

His fingers snapped around her wrist. *"Now."*

She glanced over her shoulder at the others as he dragged her away.

"How dare you!" he shouted as he slammed the door behind him. "How *dare* you disobey me!"

She began to cry.

He looked up at her in his rear-view mirror, and felt a sharp stab of guilt. He hated the fact that she didn't *really* understand…

"I'm sorry," he said, dropping his shoulders, "I'm sorry, okay? But I have to look after you. I can't let *them*…"

He stopped. What was he trying to say?

Who were *they?*

The demons, he remembered. Those *fiends* that sought to infiltrate his life, his home, his…*everything.*

Martin glared into the rear-view mirror. His reflection caught his gaze, and smiled right back.

Descending rickety steps, Martin entered Abigail's room. She was asleep, her long, delicate eyelashes fluttering as she dreamed. Kneeling down, he picked odd strands of hair away from her face, then kissed her forehead, hands, cheeks. "I'm here," he said. "Me, your Mum; always."

In his room, Belinda was curled up under the sheets, her midnight spill of hair sprayed across the pillow. He slipped into bed with her, then froze. He thought he'd heard something – a noise, coming from downstairs. Throwing back the sheets, he darted out the room and thundered downstairs.

The lounge was dark, cold, still. He checked the dining room. Nobody there. He wandered into the kitchen.

The back door was wide open.

Heart in mouth, he shut it, locked it.

Head whirling, Martin opened the kitchen drawer and snatched out a knife. He gripped it and sprinted upstairs. He shook Belinda awake. "What?" she said, blinking, sitting up. "What is it?"

"Intruders!" Martin hissed. Belinda's eyes widened. "I'll wake Abigail. Quick – into the loft! We'll barricade the door; we'll be safe up there!"

Martin charged into Abigail's room, shook her awake, shepherded her into the hall and up the stairs. She muttered and protested, but did as she was told.

In his study, he slammed the door and dragged one of the bookcases in front of it. He placed a couple of chairs on top, pulled the desk over too. "Who was it?" Abigail whispered, clutching her mother's hand. "Who was down there, Dad?"

Martin shook his head quickly. "D-don't know. Didn't see them."

Belinda and Abigail held each other as Martin paced the room. The moon was visible through the window – a bloody, lidless eye. Belinda said: "We should phone the police."

"No time," Martin whispered, shaking his head. "We'll be okay here. We'll wait till morning, then..." He stopped, ran a hand through his hair. "The most important thing is we're safe, and we're together, right?"

Abigail and Belinda nodded their heads and sat down near the barricaded door. Martin continued to pace, stepping in and out of the orange lamplight. Finally he stopped by the mirror, and his reflection's mouth cracked into a wicked grin.

Recoiling, Martin rubbed his eyes. When he brought his hand away, his reflection raised the other, and the knife glinted coldly, menacingly, ominously in the dark.

"Wait..." Martin whispered, fingers scrabbling against smooth black glass. But he was helpless, defeated, petrified.

His reflection laughed bitterly. Then it turned and made its way slowly, inexorably toward the girls. Suddenly they were screaming – pulling away chairs, grappling with the desk, the bookcase; books, papers, pens flying everywhere...

"No."

Martin's head spun. He felt a million miles away from what was going on. Closing his eyes, he tottered, murmured, swayed.

Then a black wave crashed over him, and he knew no more.

His eyes flickered open.

It was morning – sunlight seeped through the blinds like blood. Rising awkwardly from the floor, he stumbled toward the windowpane. Below, in their tidy front garden, tattered fog drifted, swirled and rolled.

Something stepped out on to the lawn. Something small, squat, lizard like.

More of them appeared: winged creatures with tails and teeth, beaks and snouts, looking up at him with myriad eyes.

Martin pressed the flats of his hands against the windowpane. "You'll never get them," he hissed, and poked out his tongue. "They're mine now. Forever."

He turned and stared blankly at Belinda and Abigail, slumped together with their hands in their laps, their heads bowed slightly, as still as statues in the early morning light.

I am the creator, he thought, suddenly, as he slumped into the chair next to his desk. He stared at the blank page in front of him, unsure of what he'd meant by that. He gazed around the room, confused, blinking into the light.

Then he began to write, and everything made sense once again.

ELEANORA

Lauren felt two things as she watched the early evening news: a painful empathy for the mother pleading for the safe return of her child, and a sudden, cloying fear that Eleanora might pay her a visit tonight.

The chime of the clock in the hall interrupted her thoughts. She moved from her armchair and stared out the window at the vacant street and filthy dark sky. Like a drumbeat, the rain rapped steadily against the pane.

"Please, whoever has her...bring her back to us..."

The mother's eyes were red-rimmed, smeared with mascara, her voice choked, desperate, scared. There was a deepthroated growl of thunder, and the picture on the television skipped a couple of times before righting itself.

"I just want to know that our little girl is all right..."

It's been fourteen days now, since Eleanora was here last, Lauren thought, *but I don't remember a thing about it.* Perhaps that was a blessing, judging from the newspaper clippings she'd found in a shoebox under the bed. But she didn't like to think too much about what she had found. She didn't like to think too much about Eleanora, either – Eleanora was so powerful, so dominant...

Another muttering of thunder. Rain streaked the windows and gushed into the drains. The mother was escorted out of the press conference with a flurry of camera-flashes. Lauren felt deeply for her, particularly now she was a mother herself. "It must be terrible to lose a child and not know where it has gone," she sighed.

It reminded her that it was time to check on her little one. She switched off the television. She could hear the rain sloshing through broken gutters, rattling the roof tiles.

As she drew the curtains, a crack of lightning scythed through the darkness, illuminating the small mounds of fresh earth in the garden.

"Sweet dreams, angel."

Lauren leant over the cot and ran a hand through the child's blond tuft of hair. The wind breathed into the room through a crack in the window, jangling the wind-chimes hanging from the ceiling. The child muttered something in her sleep. *How could anyone want to harm something so delicate, so innocent, so beautiful?* The thought made her afraid of the dark, of the television, of the clock ticking downstairs in the hall. The child turned toward her, but was still asleep, her face a perfect white oval in the shadows which played across the room.

"Love you," Lauren whispered, pressing a kiss on the child's face. "I couldn't ever do anything to hurt you. You know that."

Lightning sketched shadows across the nursery. The rain hissed a name against the window, over and over: *Eleanora, Eleanora, Eleanora...*

Lauren closed the door and drifted into the bathroom. It was pitch black there.

Suddenly, a flash.

Her face filled the mirror: skin as bloodless as parchment, black-smudged eyes, snakes of straggly dark hair splashed over bony, angular shoulders.

Then darkness again.

Downstairs, the clock ticked like a heart.

She opened her mouth to speak, but what came out wasn't her voice.

"Hello Lauren. You've got something for me, haven't you dearie?"

Lauren couldn't reply – she was curling up inside herself like a small animal in hibernation. Her fist bunched up. Then it punched glass, cracking the mirror into a web. Trembling fingers prised out a long sliver of glass, spattered with gorgeously dark droplets of blood.

ELEANORA

Thunder shook the house. Lightning washed new shadows across the walls.

Eleanora cackled to herself as she moved away from the mirror, and edged across the landing to the nursery.

DEATH'S DOOR

Rocco's was heaving. Kylie's *Can't Get You Out of My Head* throbbed over the shouting and laughter. On a gigantic TV screen, Inter Milan were playing Juventus in the Coppa Italia.

I found Ethan sitting at a small table in the corner, watching the game.

"Good match?"

Ethan shrugged. "Both teams are defending well. Vieri's fucking class, though."

I took off my coat and folded it over the chair. "I just phoned my sister. She thinks I should contact my parents."

Ethan sneered, said nothing.

Inter hit the woodwork. A group of lads perched close to our table leapt into the air.

"Christ," said Ethan, "did you see that?"

"I didn't realise you liked football," I shouted, over the noise.

He sneered. "What's that supposed to mean?"

"Nothing," I replied.

"Listen: you know what I think about your parents. So we don't have to go there, okay?"

"Sasha says they want to mend things. They want to know me again, Ethan."

Ethan stood up quickly, knocking the table. "I'm going to get a beer. Do you want one?"

I placed my hand on his. "Do we have to stay here? Jesus, you know how much I fucking hate this place."

He glared at me. In those eyes I could read exactly what he was saying: *Get the fuck off.*

I took my hand away.

Spinning around, Ethan pushed his way to the bar.

After the match, as we walked out into the night, I said:
"Sorry."
Ethan dropped his shoulders.
"It's just that...I've been thinking about my family a lot
just lately, you know?"
"Why?" asked Ethan. "I mean, after what they put you
through, you should just fucking forget them. Forget they ever
existed."
"It's not as easy as that..."
"The problem with you, Mark, is that you're too fucking
nice. You don't live in the real world. You hurt too easy.
You've got to disassociate yourself from all that stuff, know
what I mean?"
I stared at the pavement. Why couldn't I ever find the
right words to argue back?
"Hey," he said, punching my shoulder. "I want to take
you some place."
"Where?"
He smiled. "You'll see."

"What are we doing here?"
The moon shone faintly through thin, black trees, picking
out ghost-white angels, ivy-choked crypts, bent, crooked
headstones.
Ethan didn't answer. Instead, he reached into his trench
coat pocket and pulled out a bottle of beer.
"Look what I smuggled out of *Rocco's*," he grinned,
snapping off the lid, downing it. Then he stared at me, wiping
his mouth in the sleeve of his coat, nailing me to the spot with
those cold, dark eyes of his. "There's a gateway to Hell
somewhere in this cemetery."
I laughed loudly. "Sounds like something out of a Lucio
Fulci movie."
Ethan's eyes quickly killed the smile on my face. "It's true,
Mark. True as I'm here."
We both looked away, embarrassed. Everything was so
silent and still. Then he shattered his bottle against a

tombstone and said, "Come on. Let's get out of here."

Next morning I woke up alone. Washed and dressed, I walked back to the graveyard, knowing, somehow, I'd find him there. Sure enough, from behind a low-built wall, I watched him flit around all those decaying crypts and tombs and marble headstones.

I closed my eyes. My mind backtracked. I thought about the first few months of our relationship, and how everything had seemed less complicated then.

We met in a dingy bar in Old Church Street. To look at, he'd reminded me of the indie-actor Vincent Gallo, from that movie *Buffalo 66*. It was the intensity of his eyes, I guess, and the gaunt face and shock of black hair. He had these pointed ears, wore dark clothes, painted his nails and eyes a haunted house black.

I let him move into my flat with me. Before, he'd squatted in a tenement in central Portsmouth, behind the decaying Tricorn Centre. He'd look out of my window on to the rain-lashed park and garages below, and say without irony, "At least the view's an improvement."

During the first three months of our relationship, he hardly ever left the flat. He'd sit on the windowsill and stare out of that same window with such an intensity, that I'd swear he was trying to project images from his mind on to the dark, empty wastelands below. At some point the bulb popped, and we never got round to buying a new one. As a result, the flat sunk into perpetual darkness, the sun unable to penetrate the room because of the thick, dense oaks in the parkland. My job as an assistant in the local library just about covered the rent. Ethan never worked, never seemed to eat; he stole cigarettes from the local Tesco to stave off hunger.

Sometimes, in the cloying darkness of the flat, his skin would look so white that I'd swear he was a ghost. That was when I'd feel most for him. We'd wrap ourselves up in the sheets of the bed, swathed like mummies, clinging to each other, too afraid to let go.

Ethan introduced me to poetry: Blake, Keats, Rimbaud. We'd spend our days sitting at the windowsill or on the bed, reciting poetry, or listening to music on my beat-up stereo. He liked indie-rock: stuff like Nick Cave, P.J Harvey, Mogwai, Tindersticks.

Later I taught him some chords on my acoustic guitar. Pepped up by black coffee, cheap marijuana and whisky, we'd play our favourite songs deep into the early hours of the morning, or until the old woman was banging on the wall next door with a broom handle.

I loved him.

I loved everything about him.

But even in the first few weeks of our relationship, I knew that the things we'd offer to each other would push the world that little bit further away.

I opened my eyes.

Ethan had finished his tour of the graveyard and was walking home. I came out from behind the wall, feet scrunching dead leaves. He turned when he heard me, and for a nightmarish moment I thought he was a vampire, or zombie. His eyes snagged on me and he grinned. It was horrible – like the rictus of someone long dead.

Wind blew greasy hair into his eyes. "I'm close, Mark," he said.

I didn't want to talk about it. As I passed him, he said: "You will come with me, won't you. When I find it, I mean."

"Yes," I said, my back to him, "you know I would."

I glanced uneasily over my shoulder. Ethan stumbled forward, black trenchcoat swinging around his ankles. Then he clasped his cold, white hands on my face and kissed me hard, viciously on the mouth.

In the cool darkness of the bedroom I took Ethan's cock in my mouth and sucked as he stared wide-eyed, open mouthed at the ceiling. He gripped my hair in his hands and moaned, but he couldn't come.

"I'm sorry," he said, later, as we lay in the darkness together. He tried to smile. "It's like every bit of me's used up."

"Don't worry," I whispered, brushing his hair out of his

eyes. "Don't worry."

Moments later he was asleep.

I slipped out of bed and moved to the window. As I rubbed some of the condensation away with my hand, the moon grinned through that wet smear like a cracked skull.

I couldn't sleep so I read a little. As the candles dripped and dimmed, the night closed in on me. Eventually I drifted off, but my dreams were lucid and frightening. I was in a graveyard near my parents' house. My parents were standing over a headstone, Dad with his hands in his pockets, Mum clutching a wreath of dark-blue flowers. I called out to them, but they didn't seem to hear me. Soon they shuffled off, shoulder-to-shoulder, toward the gates.

I walked over to the headstone. Etched in grey marble was my name, the year of my birth, and also, the year of my death:

Mark Leighton
1974 – 2002

I ran.

"Mum! Dad!"

The wind moaned, trees creaked. Suddenly I realised I was in Ethan's graveyard – all around me were those familiar ivy-choked crypts and mausoleums with their crumbling gables and cupolas.

I caught up with Dad, tugged at his coat sleeve, placed a hand on his shoulder. As he turned, I saw that it wasn't Dad at all – it was Ethan. His face was chalk-white, and there were smudges of purple shadow around his black, black eyes.

"Disassociate yourself," he hissed, "from everything."

Ethan was gone before I awoke. I spent the day perched on the windowsill, burning through a packet of Marlboros. I thought about Ethan a lot: it was hard facing up to the fact that we were running out of things to do, to say. The romance of our squalid council flat was wearing pretty thin.

I recalled that night in *Rocco's*, days after we'd first met. We'd sat in a corner, under a green lamp and a black and white photograph of Charlie Parker. Ethan had taken me apart with his eyes, his words, his soft, melodic voice:

"Your parents are selfish, lost people. They want you to embrace everything *they* value. They crucify you because they don't understand you."

He'd reached across and laid a cold, pale hand on my shoulder.

"You should have grown up like them, didn't you know? Career-minded, money orientated, heterosexual."

Perhaps there was some truth in his words. But really he was just exerting his influence over me, and perhaps I should have realised it at the time.

You will come with me, won't you? When I find it, I mean.

What did he *really* want of me?

It was a quarter to six and Ethan still wasn't home. The sun was sinking, daubing purple shadows everywhere. I needed to talk to someone, to hear another person's voice, so I left the flat and walked up to the callbox. I punched in Sasha's number.

"Hi Mark," she said, brightly. "It's so good to hear from you. How you doing?"

I told her I was fine, but I couldn't hide the lie in my voice.

"Things aren't the same without you around," she sighed. "I went home last weekend. Mum and Dad are really frightened. They're frightened that you want nothing to do with them, and they never wanted that."

"Dad kicked me out, Sis; remember?"

"No, Mark; you chose to leave."

"I didn't have a choice! You remember the arguments, the fights we had."

"They still love you, *they've* told me that. And they blame themselves for everything. You should see them now; it's like there's a permanent black cloud over them. They can't move on. They're so sad and frail and I feel terrible for having to lie to them, for having to pretend that I have no idea where you are."

I didn't know what to say to that.

"All they want to do is talk to you," she continued, her voice softening. "Let them back into your life, Mark. Do it for me. *Please."*

As I put the receiver down, I knew I'd called Sasha at the worst possible time.

Disassociate yourself from everything.

I stared at my ghost-white face in the mirror above the payphone.

Did I *really* feel like crying?

I got back to the flat. Tacked to the wall above the bed was a note from Ethan. It read: *I've found it. Come at once. E.*

I stared and stared at it.

"I'm sorry," I whispered, shaking my head, rubbing my eyes. "I'm sorry."

I fell into the corner, then drew up my knees and wrapped my arms around them.

Slowly, very slowly, the night closed in.

I put the phone down and left the callbox. The day was dull, but the sun was trying to pierce the clouds. Sasha was coming for me in the afternoon, so I had the morning to myself.

I trudged across town to the graveyard. I clambered over broken fencing and kicked my way through the long grass and nettles. Headstones stabbed out here and there. I combed the cemetery scrupulously, just for a trace of him.

An hour or so later I discovered his footprints in some mud outside a small marble mausoleum. Immediately my chest hurt. I felt funny all over. I had no idea what it was, until I suddenly started crying. Quickly, I wiped the tears away with the backs of my hands and wrapped my coat around me.

I walked up to the door of the mausoleum. I pressed my ear against it. Then I heard him: a dead, far-off scream. I shivered. I turned away.

I paused at the gates, just as the sun came out. Light swept through the sycamore trees, picking the graveyard clean of shadow.

"Nothing," I whispered, forcing a smile. "You heard nothing."

ONE OF THEIR OWN

Hands pressed flat against the windowpane, crosses and headstones sliced through my bone-white reflection. My bed-sit overlooks Locksley Cemetery; no one visits there much.

She crept into the churchyard just after sunset. I watched, fascinated, as she flitted around a ring of decaying memorial angels. Then I pushed open the window and she looked up, moonlight dripping into her jet-dark eyes. "What are you doing?" I asked.

"Ssh!" she said, pressing a finger to her lips.

"What?" I whispered, "what is it?"

"If you're quiet, you'll *hear* them."

"Who?"

"The angels!"

She stroked the nearest white face, smoothing the lips with her fingers, the nose, the hollows of its black, empty eyes.

Shivering, I closed the window.

Soon, when full darkness came, there was nothing else to see or hear.

I dreamed that night that I was in the cemetery. The night's sky reflected back the lurid lights of the city, masking the moon and stars.

Darkness closed in, muffling the traffic, the voices from the street, the music from the bars, hotels and nightclubs.

Slowly... very slowly... a secret space was forged.

Suddenly the angels shone, their faces glowing with such an intense luminosity that I had to cover my eyes with my hands and quickly turn away.

The following night we met at the back of the cemetery, where the creepers and nettles grew wild and free. She was perched on a mossy tomb, legs dangling in the air, hair hanging limp in her stark white face.

"Aren't you cold?" I asked, gesturing to her nightie. She wasn't even wearing shoes.

"No," she replied, shaking her head, "I don't feel the cold. Not anymore."

From her mouth, ragged breath floated through the air like torn bits of cobweb. "They're not talking tonight," she sighed.

I stared at those ghost-white statues.

"What's your name?" I asked.

"Lucy."

"Where do you live, Lucy?"

She looked behind her and pointed through the tall, creaking oak trees. "Over there. I live in a block of flats just behind that old converted church." She laughed. "I'm three weeks behind on my rent, though. The landlord's going to evict me if I don't pay up."

There was a pause; wind blew dead leaves around us.

Then: "It's because you're here! They're not sure about you...they're trying to suss you out!"

I turned to face the angels again.

They held my gaze with black, empty eyes.

Beesley leaned across his desk, elbow creaking wood. He coughed, cleared his throat, fiddled around with his *Scooby Doo* tie.

"We're concerned about you, Stuart." he said. "We...the company that is, feels that you're not performing as well as you might."

Sunlight filtered through the blinds. It was too harsh, too sharp for my eyes. "You look as though you haven't slept in a week. Your shirt's creased; your hair's a mess. And your eyes...*Christ* – you look like the living dead!"

I stared at my boss. Saw how meticulously his hair was brushed to one side; saw how neatly he'd trimmed his little goatee beard. And I thought: give up, Beesley–just give the fuck up and say–*To Hell with everything!*

"You didn't listen to a word I said then, did you?"

I shifted in my seat, stared at my hands.

"Jesus." He glared down at a piece of paper on his desk. "Listen, you've some leave owed you. Why don't you start it today and take a couple of weeks off. Come back to us when you're in a better frame of mind, okay?"

I stood, pushed my chair in, and left.

"Took your time."

Grinning, Lucy stepped out from between two crumbling stone angels.

"I've brought us some whisky," I said. "Thought it might warm us up a little." I passed her the bottle. She unscrewed the lid, sniffed it, brought it up to her lips.

"I ran away from home," she said, grimacing, "hoping to find something better. But the crowds, the traffic, the noise…it frightened me near to death." She took another swig, then wiped her mouth with the backs of her hands. "Luckily, I found this place."

My eyes roamed over all those headstones, crypts and pale memorial angels. Nothing moved. It felt as though we were in some secret place, far removed from the rest of the world.

"I heard a story about this place," she said, winding a stray curl of hair around her finger. "A girl cut her own throat here. She wanted to join her boyfriend, who'd been murdered by some psychopath or other."

"Nice," I said, turning away. Trees whispered, creaked. I noticed two names etched on an old dead yew: NICK + LORETTA.

"Do you work?" I asked, turning to her again.

"I had a job," she shrugged. "As a waitress in a café on High Street. But my boss – this complete and utter sleaze-bucket – kept leching over me. One afternoon he took me aside; told me about a mattress he kept at the back of the shop. Said we could creep round there on my break, so he could show me the world and all that."

She shuddered, then pointing, said, "Look!"

I glanced at the angels. Their faces were cast in our direction. Black, broken eyes had sought us out.

"Jesus," I whispered.

She necked the last of the whisky, then cracked the bottle against a headstone. I watched her take a long sliver of glass. Then she gashed her arm, but the glass just snapped. "I don't bleed anymore," she sighed.

I talked her into coming inside with me.

We drifted up the narrow flight of stairs to my bed-sit, which was lit by a low, crimson moon. We made love on a pile of moth-eaten blankets. I brushed her hair to one side, gazed deep into her unblinking black eyes. "We can work it out," I whispered, "you don't have to go down this road, you know."

She laughed. "Oh, how noble. My knight in shining armour!"

I blushed and turned away. Then she touched my face.

Her fingers were dead cold, like marble.

"They're getting used to you," she said the next night.

Set deep within a starless sky, the blood-red moon shivered and shone. Like a dream, a strange, pale effervescence flooded the cemetery, lighting up all those decaying angels around us.

"They want to know you," she said as we watched their cracked mouths expel cold, ragged breaths.

I looked at her. She scraped her hair away from her eyes. I could see apathy there – *acceptance* – and wondered how long it had taken her to be like this.

She held out her arm. "Feel it," she said. Her skin was cold and hard. Rough. "My blood is thick and heavy. I'm tired and thirsty all the time. I'm finding it hard to think, to feel."

She looked at me. "*Listen.* Listen hard. I can hear them. Can you?"

I listened, and sure enough, I could. They were whispering, calling for her, for *me*.

She rose, then stepped back into the shadows, face stark-white against the darkness.

The moon watched.

Lucy smiled.

Then she was gone, and I was all alone.

I woke the next morning to the sun spearing through a gap in the curtains. I threw on some clothes, washed, stared at my reflection in the mirror over the sink. In the crimson light of dawn, I thought the lines on my face weren't lines at all, but cracks.

Suddenly I remembered what had happened last night, and I hurried to the window. The cemetery lay silent, drenched in the blood of the newborn sun. The angel was still there – the new angel, I mean; standing in the exact same spot where Lucy had vanished the previous night.

I sat down on the foot of my bed and touched my arm. It wasn't cold. I could feel the blood moving quickly, freely, through my veins.

"Shit," I said.

Weeks passed. I never did return to work. One rainy afternoon Mr. Beesley called around. He knocked impatiently at the door. "Stuart? Stuart? Are you there?" Eventually he gave up and left. I twitched the curtain to watch him trudge off through the cemetery under his big black umbrella.

I haven't paid the rent on this place for over three months now. The bills are mounting up. Brown envelopes litter the doormat. I suppose I should go out and get a job, make some friends or something. But I know I won't. I can't. Not now.

Instead, I wait until nightfall and then I sit outside in that strange, secret little place; in that spot which I used to call Locksley Cemetery. I watch and listen, waiting patiently for a time when they'll accept me, for the day when they'll finally take me as one of their own.

A PLACE THE NIGHT CAN'T TOUCH

I. Together Alone

*Choice excerpts from the diary of Louise Naughton,
Graveshaw, East Sussex:*

Oct 2nd

Marvin has ripped chunks out of my favourite dress. I suppose
it's my fault really – I shouldn't have left it hanging around,
though I make a point of not speaking to him for the rest of
the day.

Oct 3rd

Spent all day running around the house, making sure the slats
are nice and firm across the windows and doors. I knocked
back in a few loose nails and replaced a rotted piece of wood
over the bathroom window.

Just noticed there's a dead dog on the lawn: one of the
Creeps must have left it there. Its bright coils of innards look
like pink, wet snakes in the sunlight, and there's a real
disgusting smell to the air.

Oct 5th

While in town, ransacking the grocery store for food, Marvin
went into my room and found my beautiful, leather-bound
Hans Christian Anderson book of fairy-tales. He's ripped the
book to shreds and eaten most of the pages.

I feel angry and depressed. I can't seem to stop crying. Marvin doesn't seem to understand my distress in any way and I'm seriously thinking about muzzling him again.

Oct 6th

I've come to the conclusion that muzzling Marvin wouldn't do *any* good at all – it would be an enormous step back from everything that I've achieved with him. I've got to condition him not to do these things; in the same way that I conditioned him not to eat me!

Whilst rooting through the kitchen drawers this afternoon, I found a pad of bright, red circular stickers inside a Japanese ornate tin. I have no idea what they are supposed to be for, but I am sure I can put them to use...

Oct 16th

Last night I forgot to put my earplugs in, and in the early hours of the morning the sound of the Creeps, scratching at the slats and doors with their black, filth-caked nails, woke me.

I sat bolt upright in bed, listening to their thwarted groans above the screeching wind. The scratching intensified. Something bashed against the front door. I lit the blood-red candle next to my bed and the walls glowed a dark, dark crimson.

"You'll never get in," I whispered, over and over to myself until it became a mantra. Then, as I reached across and snatched up my earplugs, the candle hissed and spat and went out and I embraced the cold, silent darkness.

Here is a place where nothing can find me, I thought. *A safe place. A place the night can't touch.*

Oct 29th

a.m. Training is complete – I hope! This afternoon I shall conduct a little experiment to see if my hard work has paid off.

p.m. I waited, patiently, in the kitchen. Everything was carefully prepared. A little before eight o'clock, Marvin scuffed into the room looking for food. His enormous shadow enveloped the pale light on the dirty yellow walls.

Laid out upon the dining table were the remnants of last night's meal – slices of beef, cooked sausages wrapped in bacon, roast potatoes. He looked at it, sniffed, and for a horrible moment I was sure he was going to eat it. Then he turned his head and stared at the opened tin of dog food on the side.

"Go on," I said, and I indicated the tin with a slight movement of my head.

Marvin looked at me. "Go on, boy."

Slowly, he turned around. Then he lurched toward the tin and gathered it up in his clumsy hands, grunting incomprehensively as he glared at the red sticker on its raised lid. I slunk back into the shadows, gnawing my nails in apprehension. Then, as Marvin spooned his gnarled fingers into the tin and patted the processed meat into his mouth, I let out an incontainable shriek of delight. "Well done, Marvin!" I shrilled, clapping my hands. "Good boy! *Good* boy!"

Nov 3rd

The stickers are working a treat; though somehow I managed to get one on a kitchen cabinet door, don't ask me how. I walked into the kitchen just a moment ago and found Marvin with his mouth clamped around the edge of the cabinet trying to eat the thing! I couldn't help myself – I dissolved into tears of laughter.

Suddenly there was this tremendous *snap*, and the wood splintered and Marvin broke a few of his top teeth. There was blood everywhere.

"Oh Marvin!" I sighed, grabbing the kitchen-roll from off the side. "Let's clean you up!"

Marvin's sitting quietly in the lounge now, feeling sorry for himself, God bless his soul.

Nov 4th

The evenings are getting colder. Tonight, the prevailing wind rattles the loosening tiles on the roof.

I've retired to my room, leaving Marvin in his chair in the lounge, his long hands in his lap, his hollow eyes fixed on nothing in particular on the wall.

The attic window is the only window in the house that isn't boarded up and from here I can see for miles. The moon stares back at me from a cavernous sky like a sunken eye, silvering the wind-chimes hanging from the windowsill and the cars in the driveway outside. The blue Escort doesn't start up anymore, and the yellow Citroen is almost out of fuel – soon I might not be able to make my weekly run into town for food.

Earlier on I saw the Creeps loitering by the woods at the end of the garden. They looked like grotesque scarecrows in the moonlight. Perhaps I was being paranoid, but I could have sworn that they were looking straight at me... Anyway, they've gone now. But they'll be back.

They always come back.

Nov 7th

This afternoon, as I was reading an old Anne McCaffrey paperback in the lounge, I looked up at Marvin and tried to guess what his real name might be. I only call him Marvin because he kind of *looks* like a Marvin.

"You okay?" I asked him.

He turned his head to look at me, and his mouth cracked into an ugly smile.

He may be stupid and slow, but he's nothing like those Creeps outside. Not now, anyway. And I feel so comfortable around him.

He's the closest thing I have to a friend, I suppose.

A PLACE THE NIGHT CAN'T TOUCH

II. An Intrusion

Nov 9th

a.m.   Leaving Marvin to his own devices, I spent time watching the world through the window in the attic.

Under a darkening sky, the Creeps gathered ominously by the hackneyed fencing that segregates the woods from the garden. I watched them stumble and fall into one another like drunkards. Moments later the rain came, streaking down the glass like tears.

Suddenly there was a flurry of movement to the left of my vision, and I saw a young woman emerge from the woods, slipping in the mud and rain, bleeding from cuts to her arms and legs. She glanced around with wide, frightened eyes, then saw the house.

I shrunk behind the curtain.

"My God," I whispered. "This can't be real."

I twitched the curtain and looked again.

The woman scrambled over the fence, then ran the length of the garden and tried the doors to first the Escort, then the Citroen. When she found them locked, she charged toward the porch, her long dark hair whipping across her panic-stricken face, and pounded the door with her fists. "Please," she screamed, "let me in! Somebody, *let me in!*"

I felt sick, confused.

Meanwhile the Creeps poured out of the woods, staggering toward her in the grainy half-light, rain pelting their dead white faces.

"PLEASE! For God's sake, if there's anybody there, please LET ME IN!"

There wasn't time to think: suddenly I was downstairs, lifting the slats and releasing the catches to the front door. The young woman squeezed her way in, and before I could close and lock the door behind her, I caught a glimpse of a ghostly face in the gap that she left behind.

Silence.

She stood in the hall, her long, wet hair dangling in her face. "Thank you, thank you," she said at last.

I glanced at Marvin, sitting quietly in the long shadows of the lounge, and before she could look I closed the door on him.

"You...okay?" I asked.

Suddenly the girl flung her skinny arms around me and started to cry – huge, choked sobs of relief. I felt her trembling body against mine and I was scared because I knew I'd done the wrong thing.

p.m. "I'm so glad I found you," she said as we stood in the kitchen. Her eyes were black-ringed and bloodshot, as though she hadn't slept in days. "My name's Gillian. I was living in town when..." She folded her scratched arms across her chest, puffed out her cheeks, turned away.

I stared at the floor for a moment, not knowing what to say.

"What's your name?" she asked, turning her head to look at me again.

"Louise."

She smiled. "I haven't seen anyone alive for weeks! I've been living in a cellar in the old tyre factory; you know, the one opposite Graveshaw Church." She drew in a breath. "One night those things broke in and almost caught me...but I escaped."

For a moment there was an awkward silence between us; Gillian fingered a silver St. Christopher around her neck.

"What do you think happened?" she said at last. "I mean...is this some form of punishment, you know, from God? Or a science experiment gone wrong?"

I stared at my hands, as though I was searching for her answers in the creases and folds of my skin.

"My husband, Tom...h-he died suddenly six months ago. A heart defect. When I saw him that morning, standing there, in the porch...it was as if all my nightmares had turned *real*." Her eyes welled with tears. "He tried to kill me. God... *He tried to eat me*."

I began moving around the room, peeling off my bright red stickers from the dog food cans, plates of raw meat and from the fruit in the fruit bowl. Gillian watched me. I saw disorientation in her eyes. "Hey," I said quickly. "Why don't you rest a while? You look *so* tired. There's a spare bedroom upstairs, first door on the left."

"Yes," she said, nodding. "Yes, thanks Louise. I think I will."

She hesitated on her way out through the door. "Is this your house?"

"No," I said, shaking my head. "I don't know who it belonged to."

"Wasn't there anybody here?"

I thought of Marvin.

He was here.

I found him in the attic, after I'd boarded up the house.

"No. Nobody."

Gillian smiled sadly. "We're going to be okay here, aren't we? We can get through this...now that we've found each other."

"Yes," I replied, and returned the smile. But it was a false smile; it didn't reflect how utterly detached I was feeling from the world.

An hour later I crept upstairs, took my earplugs from off the top of my bedside cabinet and slipped them into my jacket pocket. Then I crossed the hall and tapped gently on the door to the spare bedroom. There was no reply, so I opened the door quietly. Gillian was sound asleep on the bed, her dark hair splashed across the pillow.

I moved to the foot of the bed and stared at her for a while. "I'm sorry," I whispered, and my words seemed to hang in the air.

You have to understand, it's not that I didn't like Gillian. It's just that I liked my world the way it was; everything was simple, there were no complications. You see, the house, this place, it's all mine, it belongs to me. It is my own private, beautiful world. Nothing can touch it; not the night, not anyone.

Downstairs, I heard Marvin move from the lounge into the kitchen.

I leaned over Gillian. Her eyelashes fluttered. Tenderly,

I touched her forehead. When I brought my fingers away, there was a single red sticker on her brow.

Marvin was clattering through the drawers looking for food when I came back down. As I stood in the doorway to the kitchen, he turned his face and looked at me with dead black eyes.

"Marvin," I said, pointing to the ceiling. "Try up there. *Up* there." He stared blankly at me. He can't read guilt, or fear. That's what I love so much about him – he can't detect any weakness in me at all. "Upstairs," I said again.

Suddenly he nodded his head and moaned excitedly and I caught a glimmer of understanding in those black, black eyes.

I stepped out of his way.

He lurched past me, then ascended the stairs. And as I heard him enter the spare bedroom, I pushed the plugs into my ears so that I wouldn't hear a thing.

HIGHWAYS

I met Lily in *The Cellar* - a dark, cavernous bar under Welch Road. As I caught her distracted gaze across the room, I thought that it had been a long time since I'd seen anyone so devastatingly attractive. Her pretty dark eyes reflected the glow of the lights, which burned like little pockets of fire in the gloom.

It took all my courage to approach her, but I needn't have worried; Lily was warm, open, funny. Turned out we'd both gone to the same primary school. We also shared an enthusiasm for Nick Cave records and Elmore Leonard novels.

"So, what do you do?" she asked, scraping her hair away from her eyes.

"I'm a wound care specialist for a medical company. Nothing exciting. You?"

Lily was a hairdresser. She owned a salon in Alverstoke Village and was doing extremely well for herself. "It's all starting to come together, you know? Like I've finally found my place in the world."

We talked for over an hour, perched together on a hard bench in an alcove at the back of the bar. Posters for clubs and rock bands peeled from the brick walls around us. It felt like our own dark cosmos: we were so utterly, so perfectly alone there.

At the end of the evening, I peeled the label off a beer bottle and scribbled my number on the back of it. "Here," I said, passing it to her, "I'd really like to do this again sometime."

A smile spilled across her face.

It made me feel like we were the only two people in the

world.

In the market along High Street, I bought a glass-framed picture of Route 101. This was on the same day that Lily moved in with me. Route 101 is now, of course, the famous Hollywood Freeway. It's the road where Norma Jean Baker posed for one of her first photo shoots shortly before her reincarnation as Marilyn Monroe. I've always been obsessed with those long, dusty desert highways; I dream of driving from Los Angeles into the Nevada Desert in one of those old convertible Cadillacs. It's a faded postcard dream I know, but I like to look at it once in a while.

I took the picture back to my apartment and hung it over our bed. Like the view of the sea through my window, it reminded me that nobody's ever really tied to anything.

"I want to travel," I told Lily as I hammered a nail into the wall. "I don't want to stay in this depressing corner of England my whole life."

Lily went quiet on me. Moving to the window, she gazed out at the black waves, crashing and disintegrating around the Isle of Wight.

"What about you?" I asked hesitantly.

She shrugged. "I've got everything I want here. My shop, my family. I couldn't even imagine leaving."

A year passed. We talked about marriage, but never got around to it. Lily's business was going great guns. To cope with the demand, she'd employed a couple of students from St. Vincent's College. But I'd grown bored with my own job; I was anxious to do something else, to escape the nine-to-five day. Lily knew I wanted to move from Gosport, and it put a strain on our relationship.

One afternoon it came to a head.

"It feels like we're pulling in opposite directions," she said, a slight air of desperation in her voice. "I'm going to stay at Mum's for a while, Dan. We both need some breathing space; some time alone."

I watched her speed off in her Fiesta, then let the front room curtain flap back into place.

I had to get out, to clear my head, so I shrugged into my coat and walked the streets. The wind was fierce, and the little knives of the driving snow stabbed through to my bones. I ended up by the river. Dilapidated fishing boats sliced out of the mire. As my eyes roamed the litter and debris beneath me, I saw something odd - something *impossible* - under Alver Bridge.

Scaling the railings, I dropped down on to the embankment and trudged slowly toward it. Waste paper blew round my ankles. I edged through thick mud, then scrambled up on to a plinth of bricks piled up in the darkness under the bridge.

The hole was about six inches in length, and perhaps an inch or two wide. I pushed my finger into it, making it real. My finger went cold, dead. I drew it out quickly, shivered, then leapt off the plinth and hurried away.

Night was falling by the time I arrived home; my apartment accreted darkness in layers, like earth piled on to a grave.

Just before ten, the telephone rang:

"We need to talk."

It was Lily.

"Yeah. I know."

"Pick me up from work tomorrow. Don't be late."

As soon as I put the phone down, there was a power cut. Everything went: lights, radio, clock. It lasted for only a few seconds. But the silence, coupled with the claustrophobic darkness, felt terrifying.

Lily worked quickly as snow pattered against the window, nattering away to the woman in the chair about last night's episode of *Friends*.

I felt a twinge of irritation.

As her last customer left, Lily locked up the salon and I drove us home. Streetlights scratched our white faces on to the darkness of the windscreen.

"Human nature fascinates me," she said, as though she'd sensed my mood in the shop. "I want to know about people, Dan. Is that so bad?"

Back home, the apartment felt colder than usual. Closing the door, I kicked off my shoes and hung up my coat. Lily switched on the TV.

"I thought we were going to talk," I said.

"I'm tired," she complained. "Can't we leave it until tomorrow?"

Walking over to the window, I pressed the flats of my hands against the cold dark glass. "I'm going for a walk then," I replied.

Outside, the snow had stopped. A brittle slice of moon emitted a cold light, fluorescently harsh, guiding me toward the river. I kept telling myself that what I had seen the other day hadn't been real.

The river reeked of tar, salt, and mud. I glanced up and down the street, then scaled the railings. Despite the night you could still see it. I wrapped my coat around me; tried to make sense of it all over again.

"What does it mean?"

The voice was thin, brittle.

I turned.

A teenager was stood on the bank, next to a discarded fridge and an overturned supermarket trolley. His face was drenched in cold, cold moonlight.

"I-I don't know," I stuttered, turning away.

That was when I noticed the crowd, congregating on the towpath above me, staring at the space under the bridge with dead black eyes.

The next day there was a quiet, almost subdued air to the office. I surfed the Internet and looked at websites on travel and tourism, just to relieve my boredom. I found pictures of Highway 101 and the US 50, and downloaded a Route 66 screensaver.

In the afternoon, I had to train up a new girl called Claire. She sat with me as I showed her how to use our computer system. She talked. I didn't.

"I've just finished a three year Economics degree at Southampton University," she told me as we waited for the computer to warm up. "It's weird how your life can change at the drop of a hat. I dumped my boyfriend on the day of my graduation. We'd been going out together for four years - well, on and off, anyway. Now, I feel great. It's so good to be free of him. God, does that sound callous?"

I shrugged, shaking my head.

"Now I know who I am, and what I can achieve with my life. The world's exciting again, like it is when you're a child."

She laughed.

Whenever the light fell into her eyes, it was like somebody dropping a stone into a pool. Highways formed and reformed; roads more exotic and dangerous than any I'd ever seen before.

Later, she said: "I moved away from Southampton to start afresh. I don't know this area at all. Perhaps you could show me around? I'd like to know what the best clubs and bars are."

She smiled at me from behind her hair. I wondered how much she meant by that.

I was home by six. As I snapped the kitchen light on, I saw the note from Lily tacked to the refrigerator: *Staying at Mum's tonight. See you soon. L.*

Nelson's was quiet. Above us, a bare electric bulb skipped and hissed, spilling our reflections on to the darkness of the window.

"You should stop trying to cling to one another," Darren mumbled, leaning back in his chair, nicotine-stained fingers drumming against the tabletop. "It's doing more harm than good."

Darren was a mate of mine - we'd worked together in the dockyards a few years back and still kept in touch.

"We're at that stage where we're too frightened to cement what we've got, and too frightened to break up," I explained. "It's like we're stuck in some kind of vacuum."

As he lit up a Marlboro, I suddenly remembered something Lily had once said – *"Even if we'd been born at opposite ends of the Earth, we'd still have found each other. Our roads would have crossed somehow."*

Darren's eyes were bloodshot. "You okay?" I asked, leaning across the table.

He shrugged. "I'm not sleeping. But it's no different for anybody else. People are retreating, hiding inside themselves. And it's not just because of this weather. They all want out."

I glanced through the window. The High Street was deserted. Litter and dead leaves flapped against the steps of the old Methodist church.

"Weird how quiet everything is," I whispered.

Darren wasn't listening. He was huddled over the table, staring into his pint.

I left my seat and walked over to the bar. As I searched my pockets for change, a crowd of people passed by the window. Their voices seemed to bring the night alive. Darren stood quickly, knocking his chair to the floor. "Come on," he said, shrugging into his coat. "If we're quick enough we can catch them."

It had started to snow again. Flakes dusted the roads. Moonlight painted the terraces, ran off them, soaked the pavement; at the base of each house was its own black reflection.

We followed the crowd through a maze of streets. There were more people at the river, standing around in small groups, or sitting near makeshift fires. Most had found a space on the bank or under the bridge itself, but figures were loitering on the road above them, their outlines sketched out by the streetlights.

"Must be hundreds of us," I breathed.

Darren wasn't listening. Brushing past me, he clambered over the railings and dropped like a stone into the darkness. Suddenly, from under the bridge, people started singing. Their voices were hesitant, fragile. Candles flickered from the darkness like a line of tongues.

An elderly man at my elbow said: "It's bigger now. It's getting bigger all the time. Reckon soon they'll be able to fit a person through it. And what then?"

I woke the next morning with a start. My thoughts were fragmented – for a moment I didn't know who I was or where I was. I sat up. From across the room, it looked like the bedroom window had cracked. But as I got up close to the glass, a cold shudder ran through me.

I wondered whether it was worth going in to work. Oddly, I thought of Claire. I wondered whether she would be there.

Even if we'd been born at opposite ends of the Earth, we'd still have found each other.

The streets were silent, eerie. The remains of the snow salted car windscreens and rooftops. I walked along a deserted Welch Road, then took the iron staircase down to *The Cellar*. The bar seemed even darker than usual.

As I walked over to an alcove, a white face peeled itself from the darkness.

"It's funny how well we know each other."

Lily raked a strand of hair away from her eyes. She was sat on our bench, sipping a glass of red wine.

I took my coat off and folded it over a chair. I wanted to ask her why she wasn't with everybody else. Instead I asked: "Has it really been two and a half years since we met here, for that very first time? I remembered thinking, *there's nowhere else I want to be.*"

I touched her face. "Why doesn't anybody *talk* about it?" she whispered, smoothing the rim of her glass.

I dropped my shoulders, not knowing what to say to that. "Do you want another drink?"

"No. Thanks. But help yourself, Dan, there's no one here. Take whatever you want."

I walked over to the bar. As I poured myself a scotch, she said: "We did see it. I mean, we're not going to fool each other over that, right? Because there's no point in *not* talking about it."

I glanced at her. She reached out across the table for her cigarettes, her pretty dark eyes not leaving my face.

"They've found other tears, holes, whatever you want to call them. In London, in Manchester. Places abroad. They're turning up *everywhere*. There's a large tear in Giza, near the Pyramids. People are flocking to them in their thousands." Her voice trembled. "Did you notice the sky this morning?"

"Yes," I said.

"What's going on out there, Dan?"

I sat down next to her. Lily put her head on my shoulder. "Everyone's going or gone," she sighed. "There's no one."

Beyond our alcove, beyond our cosmos, the darkness thickened. I couldn't tell whether it was the dark or just ...

nothingness.

"I'm here," I said, after a pause. "I'm beside you. Even if there's no one else, it doesn't matter."

I pulled her close to me and felt her tears on my skin, warm and silent.

Then we held each other for what seemed like forever, too afraid to let go.

THE DISPOSSESSED

I spent days plotting how I was going to infiltrate Kirstie Langford's life.

Each night I would gaze up at her window, at the pale, dim light inside her room, and wait for her to appear. Sometimes I'd catch sight of her – a shadow, a flicker, as fleeting and insubstantial as a ghost; then she'd turn around and vanish back into her room.

Sometimes I'd almost feel something. A residue. A trace, perhaps. Memories of Sara would re-surface: her face, her smile, sometimes even her voice.

"What are you thinking about?"

I looked up from my pint. Kirstie smiled at me. The wood-panelled walls of the Cross Keys Inn snapped back into focus.

"Nothing," I replied.

I was quiet for a moment. I rubbed my eye with the palm of my hand. "It's just… Well, this is kind of *weird* for me. To be out with you…with *anyone* like this." I painted on a thin smile. "I've been watching you for a while now."

"I know," she said.

I stared out of the window at the slate grey sky.

"This is the first time I've asked anyone out since my wife…left."

It was impossible to feel bad about the lie.

"Sorry," I said, quickly, raking a hand through my hair, "I-I didn't mean to bring her up."

"It's okay," she shrugged, and she sipped her wine. "You can talk about her if you like; I don't mind."

"She was my *everything*," I continued, staring into my

glass. "I would have done anything for her. But I just didn't see... I..."

She narrowed her eyes. "You can't let go?"

I nodded once.

"I think I understand," she said, and she looked down at her hands. "When did you break up?"

"Ten years ago. She went to Sydney, Australia, to live with another man. I tried to find her. Spent months out there, just...searching."

"My husband left me a year ago," she said quietly, and smiled.

She reached out a hand, smoothed my knuckles with her fingers.

We went back to her place.

In her room she sat on her bed as I gazed around. It was pretty much how I'd expected it to be. Old fashioned wallpaper, a small narrow bed pushed up against the wall, a pot of flowers on a desk, a dressing table. The room smelt of potpourri and a sweet, inexpensive perfume.

I looked at her, and she looked at me with lonely dark eyes. She pressed her hands between her knees. "Come sit by me," she said.

I stepped toward her. "There's something I have to tell you," I said. "I'm incapable of feeling. And I...*miss* her, you know? I know I miss her."

I stopped and took a photograph out of my jacket pocket. It was of Sara, smiling that pretty smile of hers.

"Is that her?" Kirstie asked softly. "Is that your wife?"

"Yes," I replied.

"Can I look?"

I shook my head.

There were other pictures in my pocket. Love letters, too. I took them out and laid them upon the floor beside the bed.

"What are you doing?" Kirstie asked, nervously.

"I used to be like you," I said, and I sat down beside her on the bed. "I had a good life. I have memories. No feelings, though. Not anymore."

I cast wide, vacant eyes over her. "I don't know how it happened, but I'm not human any more. I can only siphon, see. And what you've got...well, the pain makes it real, you know?"

My fingers brushed her blouse, then skin. She closed her eyes; tilted her head back. Then my hand passed right through, groping, reaching, searching the space beyond.

Kirstie's head lolled forward, eyes rolling.

It didn't take me long to find what I was looking for.

I withdrew my hand. Kirstie flopped off the bed, and I crouched down beside her, staring at all my little pictures of Sara on the floor.

Suddenly it came: the black wave, crashing over me. I glanced up at my image in the mirror and saw tears swell in my eyes. My body was shaking, my stomach churning. I scrunched photographs and love letters under me as I screamed and moaned into the carpet. Rolling on to my back, I moaned her name, over and over. *Sara, Sara, Sara.*

In time, it subsided.

I sat up, disorientated.

I stared at the photographs scattered around me.

I felt nothing again.

The police found Kirstie five days later, but by then I'd moved on, was miles away from her apartment. I made my home in another city, looking for girls weighed down by the world. It's not too hard to pick out the lonely, the broken, the dispossessed.

One afternoon I was sat in the park when a pretty girl passed by. She was tall, thin, with blond hair that made me think of Sara. As she passed, she glanced at me and half-smiled, though the smile never quite reached her eyes.

She hurried on.

I watched her for a moment, then got up and followed.

PAINTING BLIND CIRCLES

Sian laughed and reached for me.

It was early morning. The sun streamed through the blinds. I sat up in bed, blinking into the light.

"I just had the strangest dream," I said.

Sian sat up too. She stroked my hair away from my face.

"I dreamt none of this was real. The flat. Us. God," I said, rubbing my eyes, "it was *weird*."

I looked at her. "Hey, you said something just now. Just as I was waking up. What did you say, Sian?"

Sian looked surprised. "Nothing," she replied, and she smiled. "I didn't say anything at all."

I work for an insurance company in the city. I'm successful; I'm good at my job. I'm in by eight and I finish at five. My co-workers know what to expect from me, and they know what I expect of them.

Every morning, Sam, the junior clerk says: "Another day, another dollar, eh, Kai?"

A different morning – the same cliché. Naturally I laugh with him. Everything in its right place.

"Long may it continue," I told Sian.

Sian doesn't understand my approach to work. Work is work, right? You go – you get what you need to do done. Then you're free – free to become that other person, that person you repress for nine hours a day.

Sian looked horrified as I explained this to her.

"How can you do it?" she said. "How can you change your whole mindset and personality like that? Isn't it sad? Isn't it sad that you've found a way to spend nine hours of almost every day not being you?"

I thought about that for a moment, then shrugged it off.

Sian and I share a flat by the waterfront. Sian loves the sea view through the window: "It reminds me that nobody's ever really tied to anything," she said.

Sian teaches art classes on Mondays, Wednesdays and Fridays. Her own paintings grace the walls to our flat. She likes painting empty rooms in abandoned buildings best. At night, before turning in, she reads the short stories of Raymond Carver. Last year, as part of a workshop on film, she led a discussion in the Guildhall on the films of Stanley Kubrick. During the discussion, she spoke of dead space and the power of suggestion and of things which are best left unsaid.

One night I woke to find Sian sobbing quietly beside me. I touched her side. She glanced quickly at me with her pretty dark eyes and said, "Blind circles. I keep painting blind circles."

From the blank look on her face I assumed she was dreaming, but her voice, coupled with her words, left me puzzled and disturbed.

It was around the time the clocks went forward that Sian's confidence wobbled; she became needy and uncertain, and hated going anywhere without me. She spent more and more time in the flat. She lost interest in food, and as a result shrunk to seven stone. Her eyes developed a haunted look about them: there was a terrible darkness there.

One evening I brought home some holiday brochures from the travel agents. I was hoping to talk Sian into going away with me. Sian's a real home bird; hates travelling, hates straying too far from this little pocket of England. Her world is very much a closed one – anything intrusive or strange tends to overwhelm her.

I produced the brochures, and predictably she wrinkled her nose up. "Come on," I said, "where's your sense of adventure?"

"Why don't we take the two weeks here? Like we did last year. We'll lie-in every morning, go to the pub for lunch, potter around town." She smiled. "You enjoyed it, Kai;

remember?"

"You can't stay here your whole life. Surely you want to see more of the world?"

"Not really," she said.

I sighed, and switched on the TV.

"Do you think about us a lot?"

I glanced at her. "What do you mean? What's brought this on?"

She shrugged. "I was talking to Michelle yesterday; you know, my friend from college? Anyway, we were talking and I said that the bond between us – the bond between you and me – has never been stronger. It feels like I've known you my whole life."

I smiled, then brushed my fingers over her hand. "I feel that way too."

"The healing powers of our relationship are phenomenal, Kai. Wouldn't you agree?"

"Healing powers?"

"We seem to...*regenerate*."

She flushed.

"I mean, we've had our fair share of knocks, right? And in the past, we've done some pretty unpleasant things to each other."

She pulled in a breath.

"I keep having this recurring dream. We're standing on the edge of the world, right, and I know we're going to fall. It's horrible. We're holding hands, and then, suddenly, we're falling." She laughed. "It's so ... *weird*."

I stroked her hair away from her eyes. "Sounds it," I replied.

That night I dreamed I was in the corner of an empty room, fighting to breathe. I thought I was going to have a heart attack. Eventually I calmed myself down. Shadows pirouetted around me but I was definitely alone. The room smelt of dust and dead things. Gnarled tree limbs scratched against the windowpane.

I drifted over to the window. Though I was alone, I could see Sian's reflection in the cold, dark glass. I stepped toward it, then drove my fist through the pane. Seconds later I was awake.

"You okay?" whispered Sian.

She sat up on one elbow.

"You were dreaming," she whispered, and she reached out a hand to touch my face. "It was a dream, love... Just a dream."

Sian has a strange and secret inner logic which I can never quite fathom. She has lots of peculiar quirks, most of which I find endearing. She's a cleanliness freak; the entire flat has to be spick-and-span before she even attempts to leave it. If one of her paintings is askew on the wall, she'll have to straighten it out before doing anything else. And if there is a list of things to do – like the shopping, the washing, a hair appointment, say – she has to do them in a particular order or else it throws her day completely. Sometimes, though, she can be spontaneous; like the morning she asked me not to go in to work.

"No chance," I said, looking up from my muesli. "I've used up my leave, remember? And besides, it's too short notice."

"Pull a sickie."

I didn't say anything to that. She knew how I felt about disrupting routine.

"What are you so scared of?" she whispered.

When I didn't answer, she said: "You're scared of feeling anything other than numb."

"No," I said, trying to smile. "No, this isn't right. Surely we're talking about you here?"

But Sian got to her feet and stormed out the room.

That night I couldn't sleep. I paced the bedroom, then drifted over to the window. As I rubbed some of the condensation away with my hand, a thin, bloodless moon peered in at me. I let the curtain flap back in place. I glanced at Sian. Her eyelashes flickered like two black butterflies.

On top of the dresser was Sian's portfolio: I pulled up a chair, opened it up. Immediately, I was confronted with a place which I almost recognised. The place was an apartment. Furniture was lurking mounds of shadow. The moon was a smudge of eggshell white, and the shadow of the blinds looked like bars across the carpet floor.

I turned the page. In the next picture there was a person standing in the dead centre of that same room. I stared at him. That person was me. My face was cloaked with shadow, my eyes little swirls of indigo. The picture disturbed me immensely. I closed the portfolio, then slipped back into bed.

I phoned in sick shortly after eight. Sian stood in the doorway, listening in. When I put the phone down, I asked: "How did I sound?"

"Fine," she replied, smiling. "No, perhaps I should rephrase that," she laughed. "Convincing," she added, and nodded.

We sat together at the kitchen table. I ate a piece of toast as Sian tinkered with a sketch in her art pad. "So what are we doing with our day?" I asked.

She said: "I want to take you somewhere."

"Not one of your depressing haunts, Sian – *please.*"

"You need to see this one," she said, looking up. "You just need to, okay?"

She gave directions as I drove – past the Methodist church, the Guildhall, the multiplex cinema – before stopping opposite a tall, characterless block of apartments.

"This is it," she said, cranking the handbrake, pointing up at a window on the first floor. "Number 8."

We went into the foyer, then climbed the stairs to Number 8. I couldn't hear anything, except for the rain. Sian crouched down and lifted up the mat by the door. Underneath it was a small, silver key.

"Jesus," I said. "What are you *doing?* This is somebody's place."

"Relax," she smiled. "There's no one here. I've come here lots of times and nobody's turned up. It's empty, okay? Vacant."

She twisted the key in the lock. Inside, dust swirled through the air. Apart from a few items of furniture – an armchair, a sofa, a bed in the bedroom, a wardrobe – the apartment was bare. "I know this place," I said, suddenly.

Sian half-smiled, then sat herself down on the sofa. She opened her portfolio. As she painted, I remembered something she'd told me, after tearing one of her sketches in half in a fit of frustration:

"I'm never satisfied with my work. It never turns out how I want it, in my head."

The rain stopped. Gnarled tree limbs scratched against the windowpane. At some point I got up and moved to the window. I folded a blind. The moon peered in at us, and the shadows of the blinds looked like bars across the carpet floor.

When we got home, we sat at the table in the kitchen. Sian looked tired. She kept flicking her hair out of her eyes. "There's something I have to tell you," she said at last.

She fell back into her seat and closed her eyes. Seconds later she opened them again and stared straight at me.

"I've been seeing someone," she said. "A student at one of my art classes. But it's all over now. He meant nothing to me."

She slipped her hand over mine and knelt on the linoleum. "I love you so much, and it really feels like we're at the centre of something here, you know?"

She was trembling.

"You're my rock, Kai; my soul mate. And with something this good, you make an island for yourself." She ran the back of her hand across her eyes. "I'd be lost without you."

She touched my face with her fingers.

"Don't leave," she whispered. *"Please*, don't leave me."

I phoned the office from the doctor's surgery the next morning. Sam's concerned voice made me feel like I was somebody else.

"I'm just not sleeping," I explained. "I'm at the doctor's, right now."

After my appointment, I drove back to an empty flat. I looked around the place, as if seeing it for the first time. None of it made sense. I smoked a cigarette. Then I left and drove across town.

Rain crackled on the roof. I switched the radio on, but could only find static. Eventually, I drew up outside Sian's block of apartments. I cut the engine. There was just the rain.

Sian once said: *"The great thing about us is that we can change. And when we do, we do it together. It's like we're attuned to one another..."*

Sian was inside, sitting in the half-light of Number 8, painting.

"I thought I'd find you here," I said. She looked up briefly and a smile passed quickly across her face.

I sat down on the sofa. The dust was moving through the air but there was less of it now. As I glanced around the room, I noticed some of our own things: her scented candles, our books, the stereo, a pile of CDs, some clothes. She'd even hung a few of her pictures up on the bare, whitewashed walls.

Sian was different, too. She'd had her hair cut and coloured, and she wore a pretty navy dress that I'd never seen her in before.

"I'm finished with my job," I said. "I can't go back. Don't want to go back. Don't think I can face it. But with my references, it shouldn't be too hard to find something else. I've got a month or so, now that the doctor's signed me off."

I was trembling.

Sian looked up.

"That's great," she smiled. "Really great. Like you said, you'll find something."

I opened my eyes. It was dark. The air smelt of oil paints and turpentine. Sian was painting in the armchair. She looked pale and unreal, like a reflection on water.

I watched helplessly as she nicked her arm with a palette knife. Then she steeped her brush in the blood and swirled it around her palette.

Suddenly, my thoughts had a rare and startling clarity to them:

The painting was a ritual. I understood that much. It was all part of the spell. Somehow, she was controlling things.

She was controlling everything.

"Sian?"

She looked up.

"Ssh," she said, pressing a finger to her lips. "Close your

eyes. Go back to sleep. You need to rest, Kai."

My eyes ghosted around the apartment. I saw more of our things: the coffee table, a mirror, a rug, the television.

I relented.

I closed my eyes.

Later, much later, I felt the sun's warmth on my face; it streamed through the blinds, throwing threads of light on to the walls. I blinked, looked around. The armchair was empty. The room was silent. I stood, then walked over to the pictures on the wall. I stared at them for a long time. Then I heard Sian murmur, and I entered the bedroom.

She was lying on the bed, her hair fanned out across the pillow. She opened her eyes, just a fraction, and smiled at me. I sat down beside her on the bed. "That place," I whispered, "that place by the sea. You know, the one in your paintings. The ones in the front room. I know that place, don't I?"

But Sian just laughed and reached for me.

CURE

Adrian pushed his way through the hippy communes and flea-markets, his face greased with sweat. The *bazaar* was fiendishly busy – crowds bustled and swirled, wriggling under the sun like maggots. Men skulked around cattle, haggling, mopping their brows with handkerchiefs. Near a Red-Cross makeshift hospital – a yellow, decaying building on the corner where they treated the likes of leprosy and malaria – a pale-faced man leant over a stall of spices: huge archaic pots of red chilli powder and ground yellow turmeric. The spice seller smiled toothlessly, and Adrian turned and pushed on quickly through the crowd.

Eventually he turned down a street which was half-quiet, swatting at Devil Flies with the back of his hand. There were more stalls down the end of the street, but the crowd seemed to stay away. The stall-keepers lurched over their wares and watched Adrian like vultures. A few muttered to themselves as he neared. He caught sight of the strange paraphernalia being offered: Ouiji boards, monkey paws, corpse-candles, ancient books, goat-skins. One trader stood behind a stall scattered with human skulls and bones. He wrung his hands together, smiled, and said something foreign that Adrian didn't catch.

An old woman shuffled out of a doorway. She was a hunched bundle of bones as fragile as earthenware. Seeing Adrian, she shouted something incomprehensible, and he looked at her as she beckoned him into her house. He looked to the traders but they had turned away. A disembowelled goat flapped in the wind, dangling from a butcher's hook. Adrian wasn't sure what to do but he followed the woman anyway; Goa's streets were too alien and hostile and seemed merely to accentuate his depression.

Entering the doorway, he heard her calling him and he followed her up some steep stone steps. He didn't understand a word she was saying but she spoke quietly, as if she had something important to say.

At the top of the stairs, he edged down a narrow passageway. Either side of him were shelves stacked with antiquated books. He caught some of the titles, *Unaussprechlichen Kulten, The Revelations of Glakki, The Book of Eibon,* and shuddered.

He drifted into a claustrophobic little room, perfectly round and stiflingly hot. The cupboard was open and had wire mesh sides to protect the food from rodents and flies. The cupboard legs stood in bowls of water to prevent insects from crawling inside. Water, yoghurt and milk were kept cool in earthenware pots; the *tandoor* hissed in the corner. The old woman was hunched over a pot, stirring thick, dark-red contents.

"English?" the old woman barked. She turned from the pot and scratched at her face with broken fingernails. Adrian nodded. "They can't help you," she said.

Adrian looked confused. "Who?"

The old woman pointed to the window. "Them."

He presumed she was talking about the pedlars. "Oh."

The old woman began to cackle. Adrian – vaguely irritated and uncomfortable – thought to leave, but as he turned, the old woman called out: "I can help."

Adrian stopped. He could smell something coming from inside the dirty kitchen, something that overpowered the rich spices, the fish, meat. Something foreign, something dark. "What do you mean?"

"You sad." The old woman's face broke into a grin, but her eyes gave nothing away. "I know. I help." She seemed to be searching for a word. She muttered Indian to herself, then added, "You *alone.*"

Adrian shuddered. The woman was grinning. "I have to go," he replied. The woman pulled something out of the rags of her dress, a black vial which she shook up in a bony fist.

"Take," she said. "*Cure*. It help."

"What is it?"

"No more loneliness." The woman laughed. "Take." She extended her arm, offering the vial. "Drink." He took it from her. She smiled, satisfied. "Drink. Go home, drink."

He looked around, noticed charms and amulets on a table in the corner, rat skulls in the cupboard, Tarot cards on the side.

"*Go.*"

He nodded and left, taking the stone steps down to the market. Stepping into the sunshine, Adrian saw the traders watching him from behind the shade of their turbans. As he looked at them, they averted their gaze.

He rejoined the crowd. The sun climbed over mouldering buildings and rundown shanty towns. The air was thick with spices, sweat and Devil Flies. He pushed past screaming pedlars, children who seemed to laugh at him, rag and bone men collecting waste paper and empty bottles stacked outside black doorways. The heat was draining. Adrian felt his shirt stick to his flesh.

Finally he made it back to the hotel. Inside, the landlord's daughter was sitting in a chair at reception. Adrian closed the door behind him and half-smiled at her. She sat quite still, her small dark hands clasped together in her lap. As he climbed the stairs, Adrian heard her talking to herself, and he saw that she had insects crawling about inside her hair.

His room was hotter than ever so he opened the window. The noise of the *bazaar* filled the room, but he was past worrying about Goa's flying pests. The hotel was itching with bugs – creeping about in the wallpaper, beneath his bed, underneath the floorboards. Perching upon the bed, he caught sight of his own pale reflection in the mirror in the corner of the room. The black wave was coming back, crushing his spirits, draining the life from him. He stared at the bottle of Prozac on the bedside table, began to massage his eyes with his fingers.

It would be easy to construct a noose from the bed linen, to hang himself in this dark, remote corner of the world. He couldn't run any longer, and was rapidly running out of places to go. He thought about the time spent haunting the Paris Metro; the rain-swept streets of London; the ancient maggot-pits of Cairo. Stumbling to his feet, he looked down at the vial he was holding.

For a minute the world seemed to stand perfectly still.

Clasping the vial, Adrian took out the stopper and drank. There was no taste, but then, suddenly, it burnt the back of his throat. He lay on the bed, thinking about the old woman in the house at the end of the market. He could see her grinning at him, rubbing her crumbling fingers together, watching him with black, lightless eyes.

Outside, the noise of the *bazaar* faded, as though he was drifting away. He rubbed his eyes again, closed them. The world slowly began to lose all shape, structure and colour.

Take. Cure. It help.

"Adrian."

He opened his eyes. The sun was melting. The last light put up a desperate battle against the closing darkness. He sat up, rubbing his head.

"Adrian."

The voice sounded harsh and dissonant, like knives being scraped together. The windowpane rattled as the wind picked up, growling through the streets below. Adrian looked around. There was nobody in the room with him.

"You've got your wish. It's you and me now, friend."

Adrian rose and walked to the window. The market had long finished, the streets were deserted. An empty bottle rolled about in the gutter.

He sat back on the bed, the closing darkness making him tremble with a fear he had never felt before. The voice seemed so *near...*

"Don't be scared. This is what you wanted, remember?"

Adrian shuddered. Something didn't feel right. He looked to the floor and saw the empty vial. He scratched at his face, felt the sweat beneath his fingertips.

"I'm here, with you, *inside*. We're together now."

Adrian began to panic. He could feel something opening inside his skull. Something crawling out of its chrysalis; unfurling black wings...

CURE

"You'll never be alone again…"
As the voice began to laugh, Adrian screamed.

ANJA

Wind screamed, thunder rolled, rain fell sharp in my eyes. As I sprinted into Locksley Town Hall, I zipped up my coat, cuffed the rain from my face and shivered violently. I sheltered in the bustling reception area; eyes glued to the window, I waited patiently for the storm to pass.

Outside, merchants and traders bundled produce into black bin sacks, dismantled stalls and lifted heavy iron poles into the backs of vans. I listened to the hubbub of the indoor market: people buying, selling, and haggling. I smelt slabs of meat sizzled on a grill, fresh Sardinian olives, goat's cheese, farmhouse cider.

Someone tugged on my sleeve.

I turned, startled, and came face to face with a young woman with long dark hair; her pretty eyes glittered an astonishing green.

She blushed. "Oh," she said. "You don't recognise me."

"Should I?" I looked around, embarrassed.

She placed a hand over her mouth. "God," she said, blinking, "I'm *so* sorry. I-I thought you were somebody else."

She turned away, embarrassed, and I watched the rain stream down the windowpane beside us. Then, after a minute or two, she turned to me again and said, "You're a Capricorn."

"Yes," I said, narrowing my eyes. "Do I *know* you?" She shook her head quickly. "I mean, you thought I was…"

"My mistake," she said. "You look nothing like him. Close up, I mean."

"Who did you think I was?"

"A friend."

She glanced outside. "Looks like the rain's beginning to

81

ease," she said, and then, turning, "I'm Anja. I'm a Gemini. Listen, do you fancy grabbing a coffee?"

She must have seen the look on my face, because she added: "It's no big deal. Just, I haven't got a lot on and I could do with the company."

"But you don't know me."

She smiled, and I suddenly realised how attracted I was to her. "Oh, I'm a pretty good judge of character," she replied.

We sat in *La Strada*, beneath a print of van Gogh's *Café Terrace at Arles*. It turned out Anja lived in Locksley, in a small apartment above a popular Aromatherapy shop. She was in her second year of an Open University degree in Psychology, and was hoping to become an educational psychologist by the end of it.

"I'm fascinated by people," she told me. "By behaviour, mainly. I want to know how we work. What makes us tick, you know?" She flicked her hair away from her eyes. "What do you do, Simon?"

"I'm an IS engineer," I said. "I travel around a lot, fixing computers, installing new software; that kind of thing."

She nodded slowly. "You enjoy it?"

"Not really. Sometimes I feel like I'm in this rut, you know? I seem to drive out to the same places, fix the same old computers, install the same bloody software."

She laughed. "The moon enters Capricorn on Friday, so the time is ripe for change. The full moon at the end of the month signifies an emotional high tide. It's the best time to make changes, you know."

I frowned. "You believe in all that stuff?"

"I'm just...*intrigued*, I guess. Over the years I've studied astrology, cosmology, palmistry..."

"You read palms?" She brushed her hair from her face, smiled. "Do you think you could read mine? I've always wanted my palm read."

As she leant over the table, I caught a whiff of her perfume. It smelt *familiar* somehow. She took hold of my hand, dropped her gaze, and said softly, "You've got two brothers, and a sister. Your mother passed away just over a year ago."

I stared at her.

"You got that from my palm?"

Nodding, she smiled again. The smile was infectious.

Later, we went back to her apartment. It was very small, much like my own. The single window in the sitting room had the most astonishing view over Locksley. She'd replaced all the doors with bead curtains, strung up fairy lights around the front room, painted the bare walls a lurid crimson.

"What's that?" I asked, pointing to a strange prickly plant and a blackened crystal on a small, fold-out table.

"Some of my occult stuff," she said with a casual shrug of her shoulders.

We sat down on her sofa and talked. She asked all the right questions; seemed to know so much about me. Later, after sharing a bottle of wine, we made love in her bed. In the darkness she moaned and writhed, her hands splayed out on my chest, her green eyes shining at me.

That night I had this awful nightmare. I was alone in Anja's apartment. On the mantelpiece red candles fluttered like tongues. I drifted to the mirror and there, hanging in the darkness, was my own blood-red reflection. Suddenly the image changed and Anja was there, green eyes shining, face blank, body hunched. Then her hands shot out, glass shattering, and with a scream she pulled me through the mirror.

"Don't go," she said as I dressed for work. It was a couple of days later.

"What do you mean 'don't go?'" I said, searching amongst our clothes on the carpet for my jacket. "I *have* to go."

She stretched herself out across the bed. "Stay. *Please.* Phone in sick or something."

I stared at her.

She stared right back, her eyes wide, bright and cold.

I said, "Why don't we go out for dinner one night? My treat. I'll take you to that Italian on Vicarage Street."

"Sounds nice," she said as I laced my shoes. "But why can't we stay here? Just you and me, Si. Wouldn't it be great if we never have to leave this flat again?"

She sat up slowly, wrapping her arms around her legs. "Sorry," she said. "I know some of the things I say are strange. I get carried away, that's all. I don't know why I said that, about never leaving the flat." She sighed and hung her head. "You must think I'm weird."

"No," I said, shrugging into my jacket, but her glassy stare remained fixed to the floor.

It was a week later. Anya and I had arranged to meet at my place for seven, where I was going to rustle us up a meal. I left work early, was back in Locksley by six. Rain scratched discs of light around the streetlamps. I grabbed some groceries in Somerfield, and a cheap bottle of Pinot Noir. Then, just as I was leaving, I saw Helen standing under the awning outside Blockbusters.

Helen's a work colleague. She's tall, thin, with long dark hair and a bright, pretty smile. "Helen!" I called. She waved to me as I crossed the road. "What are you doing here? I thought you lived in Wickham?"

"I do," she said, "but my mother lives in Locksley. I was off today, so I thought I'd visit her."

I told her about what had gone on at work today, and about the job I had on Monday. "Do you fancy a coffee?" I asked.

"Sure," she said. "Why not."

We took a table in *La Strada* by the window. We talked a little about work, then about life in general.

"It feels like my life's gone off on one," I said as I stared into my coffee. "I had all these set goals; all these little plans. But I've lost sight of them. I mean, I wanted to be married by the time I was thirty. Have kids and everything." I glanced up at the van Gogh print on the wall. "Is that *sad?*"

She shook her head. "No. It's not sad. And it'll happen. Just don't get too het up about it." She chewed her lower lip. "Are you seeing anyone at the moment?"

"Yeah. Well, kind of. It's…creepy, actually."

"Creepy?"

I laughed. "Yeah. The things she knows about me.

There's definitely a spark, a connection, but it seems kind of...*contrived*. It's almost as though we've met some place before, you know?"

She traced her finger around the rim of her coffee mug. "Me and my bloke...well, we've been on and off for years. It's just, we get ideals in our head... Of how life should be. Perhaps we should just face up to the fact that we can never find the perfect person. It's an impossible..."

She stopped midsentence, eyes locking upon something over my shoulder. I turned. "What?" I said.

The street was deserted.

"There was a woman out there just now," she said, "staring in at us."

"Where did she go?"

"I...don't know."

"Listen," I said, reaching for my wallet, "I-I have to go." I smiled nervously. "I really enjoyed our chat."

"Me too," Helen said, nodding. "We'll have to do it again some time."

I hurried home, oblivious to the low rumble of thunder above me. Rain tore through trees, creating hypnotic patterns in puddles. As I turned down the narrow lane at the back of the garages, I saw Anja in the communal garden area just outside the flats.

"Anja?"

We stood there for a moment, staring into each other. Then she lowered her eyes and said, "Are you going to let me in or what?"

I let her in, then closed the door behind us. Anja perched herself on the foot of the bed, looking sad and forlorn. "What's the matter?" I asked.

"Who was that girl you were talking to?"

"Girl?"

"You know, the brunette. I saw you, in the café together."

"So?" I stared incredulously at her. "Her name's Helen. We work together; she's in town visiting her mum. Look, what's this about?"

"What were you talking about?"

I ignored her. Stormed into the kitchen and poured myself

85

a glass of wine instead.

Moments later I heard her bare feet pad into the room. "The first time we met," she said. "In the Town Hall. In the café. What would you have liked to have heard? How could I *really* have impressed you?"

I didn't answer.

She drew a hand across her eyes. "I've fucked up again, haven't I." Her voice trembled. "I can't help how I am. I mean…nobody else could love you like I do."

I stared at her. "We've known each other for just over a week, Anja."

She hung her head so I couldn't see her face, and laughed bitterly. "Next time," she said. "Next time, I'll get it right."

That night I had another lucid dream. Anja was leaning over me, whispering words that I just didn't understand. I could smell something burning deep inside the room. She straightened up as I blinked, and she smiled tentatively.

"Don't hate me," she said. "It's a chance to start afresh. The onus is on me, right? To make it good. To get it *perfect*."

I stared at the blackened crystal in her hand. She touched me on the face with trembling fingers. Then there was…*is*…a flash, and I…I don't remember… I don't remember anything else.

Dawn light creeps through the threadbare curtains. I'm disorientated and confused; can't even remember what day of the week it is. Flinging back the duvet, I pull on my dressing gown and drift over to the gilt-framed mirror by the door. My face stares back at me, pale, empty and scared.

Outside, dead leaves swirl across the tarmac. I wander around shops and market stalls in a daze. Above, black clouds stack over trees and chimney pots. Suddenly rain streaks my face, and I zip up my coat and dash for shelter in the Town Hall.

I listen to the rain chatter on steel drums, slosh through broken gutters, whisper against black, dusty windows. I hear the bustle of the indoor market, watch the rain outside make slow hypnotic circles in wide, dark puddles.

Somebody tugs my sleeve.

I turn, and see a face that is, for a split-second, strikingly familiar.

The young woman retracts her hand. "Sorry," she says, "my mistake." She places a hand over her mouth. Then she takes it away again and says, "I thought you were somebody else."

LORETTA

Cutting sun. Clouds twisting into shapes, places, memories. Laughter. Golden hair, slipping through my fingers like sand.

Rachel and I were out picnicking by the lakes. We'd chosen a secluded spot close to the water's edge, cast our blanket down, placed a bottle of Chardonnay into the water to chill.

The day felt dreamy, endless. We watched the sun dip in the sky, and the water and trees glow vermilion.

Just before sunset, Rachel told me about an ex-boyfriend of hers, a man she'd been engaged to a few years back.

"At the time, I thought it was love. But now, in hindsight, I know it wasn't. He had this narrow little view of us. Had everything worked out, you see. Where we'd live, what I'd do for a living, what sort of car we'd drive. Jesus, it was scary."

She sat up, her hair sliding across her face.

"With him I was a closed book. I thought that was how it was when you're with somebody: you both have your secrets."

Suddenly something surfaced in her pretty green eyes – something dark, something screaming. "Promise that you'll keep *nothing* from me. Promise me, Nick."

In the gloaming, a shadow was watching us from the trees.

"What?" she said.

"Nothing," I whispered, reaching out quickly to touch her face. I forced a smile. "Nothing can tear us apart. I've always said that, haven't I?"

I came home from work, hung my coat up on the banister and

entered the living room. The shadow was there – lurking in the corner behind the settee. I stared at it as Rachel called to me from across the room.

"Good day, love?"

I couldn't answer.

She reached over the coffee table for her cigarettes. "Do you fancy a glass of wine? I'll open up a bottle, hey babe?"

She got up.

The shadow followed.

As she poured the wine, I watched the shadow reach out and stroke her hair with the back of its hand.

"What's the matter?" I asked as she froze.

Rachel looked quickly at me, then away again. "You thought the world of somebody," she said at last. I opened my mouth. "It's all right," she said, "I understand. It's nothing. It really isn't."

I went out that night with Mike, a friend from work. We went to our usual haunt, *The Porter*, a small, quietish pub on the edge of town. After a couple of pints, I told him about what Rachel had said.

"Sounds like you're both as insecure as each other," he sniffed. I stared at him. "What? Stop looking at me like that, Nick. You know what I mean." He shot me a knowing look, then slotted a Camel between his lips.

I dropped my shoulders. "We're doing okay. We're making a real go of things. I think I'm happy."

"I'm pleased for you," he said, "really I am. Rachel came along at the right time for you."

I thought about that for a moment. Then Mike said: "So I take it you told Rachel about…"

I shook my head. Loretta's gone and that's that, I said.

"But don't you think you should?" he pushed. I sighed and looked away.

He leant over the table. "Stop being so *hard* on yourself. In the end you chose life, and that's good, right? It's okay to talk about it, Nick. And you've got Rachel now, remember?" He placed a hand on my shoulder. *"There's nothing wrong with you."*

He smiled. It helped.

I was home by midnight. I closed the door, kicked off my shoes, hung my coat up on the banister. The house was dark. It felt like nobody lived here at all.

Before I opened the bedroom door, I felt sick and scared. I pressed a hand to my mouth. Then I took it away again and pushed open the door.

The bedside lamp was on, but the bed was empty. The window was open, a breeze ruffling the net curtains.

"Rach?"

As I walked back out on to the landing, I noticed the spare bedroom door was ajar. I found Rachel inside, sitting cross-legged on the floor. All around her were paperbacks, magazines, shoeboxes of sentimental trinkets, photographs, a pack of Tarot cards. Stuff that I'd shoved away and forgotten about.

Beside her the shadow whispered, hand cupped over her ear.

"Rachel!"

My voice broke the spell: she blinked rapidly and looked down, confusion spreading all over her face.

I snapped off the light. The darkness took everything away.

That night I knelt beneath the wings of a stone angel.

I felt the breath of my lover in my ear, then a cold white hand over my mouth. *"Swallow them."*

I glanced quickly at the girl with kohl-smeared eyes and black hair, then up at the angel.

There was vomit all over it.

I woke sweating, gasping, panicked. I looked frantically around. Rachel was asleep. From out of the darkness the shadow moved toward her and I sat up on one elbow as it loomed over the bed.

"Stop," I said, but it was too late…

With a black, flickering hand, it touched Rachel softly on the brow.

During our lunch break, Mike and I went to the café across the road. As he chain smoked, I told him about the shadow: "I know who it is," I said. "It's Loretta. She's found a way back to me."

Mike stared and stared. "You're not making any sense, Nick."

He leant across the table, leather coat creaking. "It's a guilt thing, right?"

I laughed; it sounded pathetic. "I made a promise," I said. "I made a promise I didn't keep, Mike."

When I got home, Rachel was all alone in the living room. The lights from passing cars outside swept across her empty face. I took my coat off and went to her. She turned to look at me, then wrapped her arms slowly around my neck.

Suddenly her eyes changed colour – *green to black*. I pulled away. "What?" she said. "What's the matter?"

I screwed my face into my hands.

"You're not her," I whispered. "You're *not* her."

I woke suddenly the next morning to the sun spearing through the threadbare curtains. I turned over. Rachel wasn't there.

I dressed quickly, then ran downstairs. She was in the kitchen, staring at a photograph on our tiny, fold-out table.

"What have you done?" I said.

Her straight hair was cut short, dyed midnight-black, and she'd smeared thick black kohl around her bright green eyes. She glanced up at me as I came in, then back down at the photograph on the table.

"You never once mentioned her to me," she said. "And the thing is, she was *always* here. Right from the beginning. It kills me, Nick. I can't compete with that. With what you shared."

I looked at the photograph.

How did she find it?

No: the shadow found it.

Loretta.

Loretta was grinning up at me now, smiling that strange, warped smile of hers.

"This is *exactly* how she wants you to feel," I said, shaking.

"You broke a promise," she whispered. "You broke a promise, didn't you, Nick."

She stood slowly, chair legs scraping the floor. Her eyes changed colour. Green to black. She smiled. The smile was all wrong.

"This time," she said, "you'll get it right."

It's an hour's drive to the graveyard – the graveyard where our names are etched on an old dead yew; where we made our pact beneath the eyes of a crumbling stone angel.

It's raining: sheets of it cut through the trees, turning the ground to slush. Hand in hand we flit through the graveyard. Trees thrash. Leaves dance.

We stop beside that stone angel. Its face is blank, decayed, gone. One of its wings has broken. We kneel beneath it.

She reaches into her pocket and takes out the bottle of sleeping pills. She twists off the lid, shakes them into the palm of her hand and presses them into my mouth. I gag, but still she presses. With one hand over my mouth, she tilts my head back. "Swallow them," she hisses.

I swallow. She presses my face into her chest and I weep soundlessly. Running her hand through my hair, kohl bleeding from her eyes, she kisses me softly on the face.

And here, in this dark little pocket of the world, I am finally reunited with my love. For she has come back to me. My lost love.

Loretta.

THE NIGHT IS MINE

"Come on," she said, "start the engine."

Heather had brought me to the B&Q car park. It was late evening. Dead leaves ghosted across the deserted industrial estate.

I groaned. "Do we *have* to do this? I'm *tired,* Heather."

"You promised, Majid."

I turned the ignition key. The car coughed, then growled into life. I knew Heather got off on this, on being in charge. It was her chance to get one over on me. But that was Heather; she had to be in control, constantly.

I stalled the engine, the car rolled. "Shit," I said, cranking the handbrake.

"Take it easy," she sighed.

"You're enjoying this, aren't you."

She shook her head. "Don't be so childish, Majid."

I felt helpless; out of control. And as I drove her Citroen around in slow, stop-start circles, I wanted Heather to *understand;* I wanted her to feel this way, too.

She said: "Let's try it out on the roads tomorrow."

"Whatever."

She clucked her tongue. "Don't get like that."

"Like what?"

"You know."

She drove us home in silence. Night had settled. I felt less uncertain, more...*alive.*

"Why can't things be *straight forward* between us?" she said as soon as we got in. She slumped into her armchair and glared up at the stopped clock on the mantelpiece. I didn't know what to say to that.

Shortly before eleven, we went to bed. Heather fell quickly to sleep, but I was wide awake. As her eyelids fluttered, I leaned over her and drew back a flap of hair from her ear. I spoke of hidden worlds, of distorted roads; of the quiet, black spaces we inhabit alone:

"We can't escape," I whispered. "All we should ever want to explore is each other," and then I stilled her eyes with the tips of my cold, trembling fingers.

Heather was in the back room, scribbling numbers into an A4 notebook. "How's it going?" I asked, tentatively.

"Not good. We're going to have to tighten our belts for the next month or so."

I knew what she was hinting at, so I retreated outside, into the garden. I leant against the rickety patio fence, smoking Camel after Camel. Trees fell into each other, chuckling darkly into the wind.

Suddenly I remembered something Julian had said, in a smoky, dingy pub in Locksley town centre:

"What makes you think Heather will never leave you, Majid?"

"Because," I'd replied, confidently, "she's too afraid of being alone."

I blinked, then glanced quickly at Heather through the open patio doors. I knew what she really wanted me to do was to sit with her, so that we could work things out together. But I couldn't do that; it just wasn't me. "Leave it," I shouted. "Let's watch TV. I'll make popcorn; what do you say?"

She didn't answer. Sighing, I threw my cigarette to the floor and stamped on it.

Later that evening she joined me on the settee. "Do you think you could do some shopping for me?" she asked.

"Sure."

"I've made a list of the things we need. It's out in the kitchen."

"Fine."

She shifted in her chair. "What else will you do tomorrow?"

"I'm not sure."

"You're not sure?"

"I haven't really thought about it."

She was quiet for a moment. Then she scratched her face and reached across the table for her cigarettes. "It must be boring," she sniffed, "hanging about here all day."

"I like it," I said, picking up a book.

"We really could do with you working."

I fell silent.

She sighed heavily. "You've always been so fucking passive, Majid. What if I decide tomorrow I want to give up work? We'd lose the lot: the house, car, *everything*. Doesn't that frighten you?"

"No," I said, shaking my head, "no, I don't think it does."

"Well," she replied, "it frightens the fuck out of me."

People say you're not complete unless you own a car. That's bullshit, though. Heather believes it, and since the start of our relationship she has been pestering me to take driving lessons.

"It completely epitomises you," she'll say, "the whole not-wanting-to-learn-to-drive thing."

Heather loves driving; she passed her test at seventeen. "It's a rite of passage," she explained. "Passing my test was the most important thing I have done in my whole life. It opened up *so* many doors. You can go anywhere, do anything. *Be* anyone."

Her dream is to drive America's long, clear highways, through dust ball towns and deserts. Her favourite album is *Nebraska* by Bruce Springsteen; she listens to it late at night through the headphones of her Discman: "I can just visualise the interstate routes, the strip bars, the fast-food joints, the small businesses and the diners. You can almost smell the air of broken promise, Majid."

During the day, Heather teaches primary kids in a small school in Locksley. "The very thought of helping to shape people," she'll say, "to try and bring the best out of them; well, there's no bigger kick than that." She spends her weekday evenings planning lessons. I admire her dedication, I really do, but she does too much; she puts needless pressure on herself. It was like last year, when she joined a local community group to picket in East Knell Common. Property developers wanted to bulldoze the pretty brook and woodland there. I barely saw her for weeks on end. "It's just something I have to do," she told me. When she saw the look on my face, she added: "Forget it. You don't understand. How on Earth could I expect you to understand?"

I love Heather. And I know she loves me, in that strange, awkward way of hers. She often says she doesn't understand me, and that I make things hard for her. But it's only because, ultimately, she's insecure about herself.

"The most important thing," I'll say, "is that we're together. Nothing else matters."

Words are rarely enough, and occasionally I have to *show* her. It's not *controlling;* I'm just reminding her of the truth, you see. Of what's important. Like the night when some friends of mine were having a house warming.

"I don't have anything in common with your friends," she said as she rifled through her wardrobe looking for a dress to wear. "You'll all be talking about the past, about moments you shared together, and it'll make me feel *alienated.*"

"We won't have to stay long," I argued, shrugging into my coat. "All we need to do is show our faces."

Julian's house used to be an old Methodist church; it was hunched and decayed and overlooked a dark, unkempt graveyard. Strange looking trinkets, wind-chimes and charms jangled from the front porch. A black cat watched us from the weed-strewn garden as we pulled up.

"Come in, come in," Julian grinned as he opened up the front door. He introduced Heather to his latest girlfriend, Laura; immediately, the two of them started talking. I left them to it and followed Julian into the kitchen.

He opened the fridge. "I heard you went to Alex's thirtieth last month," he said, tossing me a Bud.

"Yeah," I nodded, "you missed a pretty good night there."

"How's things going with Heather?"

"Oh, you know her; she likes to think she's *so* independent, so self-assured." I laughed. "Sometimes she completely forgets that she needs me."

"Heather is wrong you know," he said, suddenly. "There *are* other worlds besides this one."

I stared at him.

"Did you get those books I sent you?"

"Yeah," I said, ruffled. "They're good."

"Tried anything out yet?"

"One or two things."

He nodded, grinned. "It's good to see you again," he said, patting me on the shoulder. "I'm glad you're doing okay."

I knocked back my beer, took another one, then went searching for Heather in the lounge. Couples laughed as they danced and groped in the darkness. I bumped into Scott, another friend from college; he was whispering into the ear of a girl I didn't know. As I tapped him on the shoulder, he straightened and I caught sight of the girl's vacant, staring face. "Have you seen Heather?" I shouted.

Scott shook his head vigorously. "Think she went upstairs," he replied.

I hurried up to the first floor, tried the first door I came to, and slipped into a cold, ill-lit room. I looked around, noticing a Ouija board propped up against a table. Julian was by the window, his face stained red by a lava-lamp. Laura was on her knees, licking a cut on his palm. She didn't acknowledge me in any way. Julian winked at me and I quickly turned away, embarrassed.

Heather was in the next room, staring blankly out of the window. She had the flats of her hands pressed up against the pane. "Heather?" My voice was hesitant, frail, cracked.

She turned slowly. "I don't think I like any of these people. I feel out of place, Majid. I told you I would." She rubbed her eyes slowly with the palms of her hands. "I'm tired. I'm not sleeping well. I keep having these dreams about…well, spooks and things." Her eyes lifted to my face. "Sometimes I dream you're talking to me, but I don't understand…"

I cut her off. "Come on," I said, grabbing her wrist, "let's have a drink. Then we'll make our apologies and go."

Neon and halogen glowed like dying stars through the dark of the windscreen. Above us, the cracked moon was obscured by office blocks and three-storey townhouses. Heather rubbed her brow as we waited at yet another red light.

"You okay?" I asked.

"Think so," she muttered, turning to me. Then the light flickered to green and we were away again. As we left the city behind, the moon grinned down on us like a death's-head.

"Where are we?" I asked.

Heather didn't answer. She blinked and craned her head to read a skewed signpost pointing back the way we'd come.

"Shit," she said, "I think we've gone wrong somewhere." She dropped her shoulders. "I've lost all sense of direction. I know these roads like the back of my hand, but tonight they're alien to me, Majid. I *swear* they've changed."

"Pull over. I'll get the map out the back."

As soon as she pulled into a lay-by, her breathing altered. I thought, *it won't be long now.*

I switched on the little yellow light and unfolded the map over my knees. "I can't work out on here where we are."

"We're close to Locksley," she said, "I *know* we are. I recognise certain places – like the post office and that old white house back there. But the roads don't go the way I expect them too." She smacked the steering wheel with the palm of her hand.

"Hey," I said, "calm down."

She blinked tears. "I don't know what's happening to me, Majid; I really don't."

She pulled out of the lay-by. Two minutes later, she said, "It's okay now. I know where we are. This next road will take us into Locksley High Street." She flicked the indicator and turned left down a dark country road.

Moments later she was in tears. "No," she said, shaking her head, "no, this isn't right."

"What? What isn't right?"

"I don't know where we are! I'm going mad, Majid; I'm going fucking crazy!"

She pulled over, her breathing fast, shallow, and ragged. She couldn't talk, only pant and cry. I smoothed her hair out of her eyes. Then she reached for me, fingers scrabbling at my coat, and I held her in the darkness as she trembled and wept in my arms.

It's the early hours of the morning and we're sitting, dead still, on the edge of our bed. Heather's exhausted; her hair hangs limp in her dead white face.

I speak of hidden worlds, of distorted roads, of the quiet, black spaces we inhabit alone.

"We can't escape," I say. "All we should ever want to explore is each other."

Heather is half-asleep, barely conscious. Her hand scrabbles around, finds mine, and my fingers close quickly around it.

In the cold light of day she'll find herself again. She'll push this to the back of her mind; try to take control again. But for now, the night is mine.

"All roads end here," I whisper. "Together, forever. It's like we always said, Heather."

She looks up, moonlight painting her blank face white. The moon through the pane is gouged and scarred: a roadmap of disintegrating highways.

"Yes," she whispers, "forever," and I close her eyes gently with the tips of my trembling fingers.

ALL WE HAVE

1

She woke up, naked, covered in blood. *Who am I?*

She scraped gore-spattered hair away from her eyes. *I'm Jennifer*, she thought; *I'm forty-two years old.*

She was in the main room of a small apartment, sparsely-furnished with a big expensive sofa, books on lifestyle and health balanced on the arm, an oriental rug draped across the floorboards, a coffee table, and a large widescreen television.

"Hello?"

Startled, Jennifer spun around. A man stood in the corner of the room, dripping gore all over the carpet. "Where did this shit come from?" he said, wiping a film of blood away from his face with the palm of his hand.

Shivering, she ran into the next room, a bedroom, and slammed the door shut behind her. She ransacked the drawers, threw clothes out on to the floor, wiped the blood off her face with a towel. Then she pulled on some jeans and a sweater.

The man knocked quietly at the door. "What?" she called, sitting down quickly on the bed.

"May I come in?" He poked his head around the door. "I just thought..."

"Who are you?" she asked, her voice breaking, breathless, panicked.

"I don't know," he replied, shrugging. "I mean, my name's William and I'm forty-five years old. But, I don't know... I...I don't remember anything else about myself."

"You're married," she said, nodding at the band on his finger.

"So are you."

She glanced at her own finger to see a plain silver ring. "Oh," she said, absently.

She bit her lip. "What do you think happened in that other room? You don't think…"

She stood up quickly.

"Where are you going?" he asked.

"I…I have to get out of here."

"But don't you think we should puzzle this out together?"

She shook her head. "Sorry, but I have to go. I need some time alone to think about all this. Okay?"

2

The sky was pitch-black. Like a moth, Jennifer flitted toward distant lights, stumbling into a tall, narrow, rickety hotel. "The Eden Inn," proclaimed the buzzing neon sign. As she hesitated on the threshold, the reception door slid silently open.

"Can I help you?" came a dry voice from behind the mesh window of the proprietor's booth; the occupant's eyes gleamed like polished black marbles. He had a distinctly ophidian aura about him.

"A room," she whispered, glancing timidly about the sterile, empty reception area. He nodded slowly, reached for a key. For a second, the metal head of the key resembled a grinning skull, but then appeared completely normal when she looked more closely.

Realising she needed money, Jennifer frantically searched the pockets of her jeans. To her relief, she pulled out a small canvas wallet, and there was money inside. Breathing quickly, deeply, she slid a couple of notes under the wire mesh, grabbed her key, and hurried up several steep flights of stairs to her room on the top floor.

Room #666 was small and dingy. It had a bed, a chair, a little table, and a Goya print, *Asmodeo,* nailed to the wall. The window had a crack in it, and the ceiling, a smudge of mould.

Jennifer kicked off her shoes and walked over to the mirror by the door. Yanking a cord, a humming striplight splashed her reflection on to the cold, dark glass.

She looked frightened, and felt weak and morose. Wondering whether this was part of her fabric, her make-up, Jennifer retreated to the chair by the window and sat down. The window was a square of impenetrable darkness; it was as if somebody had draped a black sheet over the glass to screen her view of everything but her own now shadowy reflection. This made her reconsider her situation, and decide that she'd made a mistake in trying to solve her dilemma alone.

Sighing in frustration, Jennifer gathered up her things, puffed out her cheeks, and left the room.

3

"Hullo," said William, cautiously, opening the door. "I was wondering when you were going to come back." He held the door open for her.

She paused in the threshold for a moment or two, uncertain, then gingerly entered the room.

They sat down together on the sofa, flicking through a photograph album he'd found. "I'm glad you came back," he said earnestly. "There's so much we have to talk about."

"Jesus," she whispered, staring at a photograph of a young woman in a pleated pink skirt. "Is that...*me?*"

"Like my pastel-blue bellbottoms?"

Her eyes skipped to the next photograph. "That's you?" She laughed hysterically. Then, just as quickly, her face paled and she stared at her hands. "How long have we...?"

William shrugged. "I reckon at least, what, twenty years?"

"Twenty years?"

"I found a box in one of the drawers. It's full of our old love letters, anniversary cards, photographs; sentimental stuff, you know..."

He dropped his hands into his lap. "Come with me," he said. "There's something I have to show you, in the bathroom."

She followed him into the little room next door. It was dark. He yanked the cord, and she stared disbelievingly at the contents of the bathtub.

"What the *fuck?*"

There were flesh-covered gloves with nothing in them,

shredded torsos and pale, floppy tubes that used to be arms and legs, fingers and toes.

"I salvaged them from the other room," he said reverently. He folded up his shirtsleeve.

"Christ," she said, pointing. "Is…is that a *face?*"

He pulled the indicated item out of the bathtub, draped it over his skull, patted it against his flesh. "Look—a perfect fit!"

"Jesus."

He looked at her then, through the mask of flesh hanging from him. "There's another in here somewhere – I think it's yours…"

4

"Something happened to us," he said, later, as they sat perched on the edge of the bathtub. "We shed…came apart." He tapped his foot against the linoleum, scratched at the whiskers on his chin. "I don't know how or why. But you should have seen the state of our front room. As I was cleaning, I found smashed plates, torn letters, broken LP's…"

"Listen," she said, "I don't *know* you. Hell, I don't even know *me!* I'm scared, William…really fucking scared."

"We don't have to be alone…separate," he whispered softly. "I mean, we can figure this out, right?"

Jennifer glanced uneasily at the contents of the bathtub. "This place," he continued. "Well, it's the key to our past—to our identities, *to what we are.*"

"To what we *were*," she sighed.

"Will you stay? Please?"

She looked at him, then got up and drifted over to the window. She pulled back the curtain. Outside, the sky was still black and strange and starless. There was just her reflection, frightened and alone, hovering in the black, black pane.

William was right. Whether this was Heaven or Hell, it was all she had.

He placed a hand on her shoulder…gripped it.

"We once said *forever*," he whispered, and smiled hesitantly. "Remember?"

THE ART OF DRIVING

Sometimes, when the world feels too wrong, I hold Helen tight and tell her that I love her.

We've been going out for five years now. Practically married I guess; or so my friends tell me. We live in an apartment on the outskirts of the city centre. It's quite an old apartment in an old block of flats. Very classic, Georgian style, with high ceiling, pillars and a balcony. I suppose we function as a couple quite well. We rarely argue and we're not scared of silence. You know how it can be tense sometimes between a couple; well, it has never been like that with Helen and I. We're comfortable sitting in the living room without feeling the need to talk. We have a rota tacked to a drawing board out in the kitchen. We divide the time equally between ourselves so we know whose turn it is to wash up or do the gardening or take the washing to the laundrette. It's important to have a routine. We plan every hour of our weekends so we can make the most of our time together.

I watch Helen sometimes and try and guess what she's thinking. Helen has long dark hair and a pretty smile. I know that all she wants is to be secure, and I can give her that security. I've just been promoted in my job. I'm now an official team leader in a busy building society in the city centre. By thirty I hope to be a managing director of the company. I know I have the determination and motivation to succeed. I'm not scared of the thought of marrying Helen; I'd like children someday. I'm not sure how Helen feels about this, though. It's something we haven't ever talked about. Helen's just a nice, ordinary person, somebody who's dependable. I think I know everything about her, though every now and then she'll surprise me, like the day she asked me to teach her how to drive.

Helen had never shown interest in driving before. As far as I knew, she hated travelling. Yet in our bedroom we have all these pictures of romantic places she dreams of exploring: deserts, beaches and highways I had never heard of before, from Australia to Africa to the South of France. She loves films like *The English Patient* and *The Sheltering Sky,* just because of the exotic places and cinematography. She grew obsessed by early R.E.M. records like *Reckoning* and *Life's Rich Pageant* because the band wrote the songs while they were on the road, touring small American Deep South towns. Helen romanticised about going to faraway places, but I couldn't get her to travel. I was going to drive her to the Dordogne in the South of France last June, but she got cold feet and didn't want to go. Helen doesn't even like me driving her to the shops. She walks to places she has to go, even to work. She's a real home bird, which strikes me as strange for somebody who's so obviously in love with mystical routes and romantic places. She has a phobia for buses and trains and aeroplanes. Once, she told me about the time she'd had a panic attack on an over-crowded bus. She has never been on a bus since.

I took her to a barely used car park close to the large DIY superstores, a couple of miles from the flat. It was early evening. She drove my Escort round in circles, familiarising herself with the controls. Dusk closed in around us. I remember looking up and seeing our pale reflections floating in the darkness of the windscreen.

"So what made you want to do this?" I asked as I rattled through the glove compartment looking for a CD to play.

"Don't know," Helen shrugged, half-turning, her eyes still fixed on the road ahead. "Just need to prove to myself I can do this. I woke up this morning and felt like an entirely different person."

That night I saw Helen sleepwalk for the first time.

As I woke, I knew something was wrong. The door hung open. Sitting up on an elbow, I looked wildly around. Helen was gone and I was alone. For some reason I was drawn to the window. First I saw my white reflection, then somebody dashed through the darkness directly beneath me. Our apartment overlooks our garden, and a tangle of overgrowth behind the rickety back fence. There is a churchyard behind the wild foliage and then there's the busy main road. I knew whoever was out there was rushing through the thickets and wild creepers and heading straight for the churchyard. In a flash of recollection I saw dark hair and a pretty white nightdress and realised it was Helen. I quickly dressed and followed her outside.

The wind moaned through the trees. Kicking my way through rotting clapboard fencing, I ventured toward the churchyard. The lights from passing cars and streetlights shone like stars through the enveloping darkness. "Helen!" I called.

I saw her in the distance, standing close to the main road, encircled by white gravestones jutting at angles from the earth. She was staring at a memorial sculpture of an angel. I approached slowly, careful not to take my eyes off her. She didn't flinch as a juggernaut thundered past, rattling the hackneyed fencing and trees, barely five metres from where she was standing. I stood close to her and she was just staring straight through that statue. She didn't look right.

"Come on, let's go back," I said. She looked so pale and distant, like a reflection on water. I didn't want to touch her at first. I imagined her skin so deathly cold. *This isn't Helen,* I remember thinking, *this is somebody else.* I slipped my arm around her and heard her sigh.

The statue glowed faintly in the darkness. I saw blood splattered over the serene marble face. Slowly, I led Helen away. "It's okay," I soothed, "it's okay."

Once we were indoors, I laid Helen on the bed. I checked her body, but could find no trace of any cuts or wounds. She curled into a quarter circle. When the morning came, it felt like none of it had ever happened.

"You went sleepwalking last night," I said. She looked up from the television, startled.

"I what?"

"You walked all the way outside and stood in the

churchyard." Helen stared at me. "Honest."

"Jesus." She ran a hand through her hair.

"Have you done it before?"

"A couple of times. When I was a kid." She frowned. "Are you bullshitting me?"

"Honest to God. You went sleep walking."

Helen looked at her hands for a while, then at me. "I haven't done that since I was a kid."

"Did you do it a lot when you were a kid?"

"The odd occasion." She started to laugh. "God, I'm sorry."

"What for?"

"I never did tell you about my sleep walking habits, did I?" I shook my head. "I used to sleep walk whenever I was really worried or stressed about something. Like when I was ten and my grandfather was dying. I walked every night he was in hospital, right up until he passed away. My parents were horrified. They took me to the doctor's and everything."

"You okay?"

"As far as I'm aware," she smiled, "I'm fine."

I reached across and took her hand. It was the closest I felt to Helen in a long time.

A couple of days later, I was driving back from work in the rain. The sky was grey and empty and the rain drowned out the music playing from the local radio station. I was winding down after work. I'm a different person there, you see. I have to be. I'm much more assertive, less emotive. I slip into a different mind-set as soon as I step into the office. As far as I am concerned, my life with Helen takes place in another world.

I stopped at traffic lights and looked up into the mirror. Through the rain I saw Helen. She must have been walking home from work. She was standing in a shop doorway, the rain blowing her hair into her face. She hadn't seen me. She was laughing and talking to a man I didn't recognise.

The traffic lights turned green and I eased my foot down on the accelerator.

Back home, I paced the apartment and stared at my sallow face in the mirror. I couldn't get the thought of Helen talking to that other man out of my head. Was she having an affair? The more I thought about it, the more feasible it became. Her recent change of demeanour had struck me cold; it was as if I didn't know her anymore.

The next day I left the office for lunch and sat in the rest room. There was a bundle of magazines scattered across the coffee table. *Heat, Cosmopolitan, Sugar, Hello.* I flicked through random magazines, trying to locate a face similar to the man Helen had been talking to. I don't know why, but I had to clarify the image. Five minutes before I was due to resume work, I threw the magazines down in frustration.

I came back the next day with a pair of scissors I'd smuggled out of the store cupboard. I cut various faces out of the magazines and rearranged assorted parts until I had a collage that half-resembled the face that haunted me. A bridge had formed, connecting my two juxtaposed worlds.

Then Cassie came along, and I could see some kind of light at the end of the tunnel.

She was nineteen. She'd just joined the company as a switchboard operator and I was her supervisor. I talked to her in my office about standard office procedures and she kept smiling at me and stroking her hair. She caught me looking at her while she was on the telephones. One day Cassie came into my office and gave me the weekly statistics. Our hands brushed and it felt electric. I'd go home and sit with Helen and I'd try and listen to her whenever she felt down or tired but all I could think about was that nineteen-year old. I knew that if I had the chance I would fuck Cassie, because that would somehow make things right in my mind. I wouldn't care what Helen would say or do when I wasn't around; I would have been with Cassie.

So I asked Cassie out for a drink and we went to The Tap Room one Thursday lunch hour. It's quite a large bar in the centre of the city, about a five minute drive from the office. We sat on high stools drinking cocktails. The bar seemed extensive because the walls were aligned with tall mirrors. Every time I looked around I saw me and Cassie, and that image of us together seemed so unreal. A sign advertising a beer flickered above the bar – reflected in the silver mirrors it

111

made a tunnel of light spiralling away into infinity.

Cassie wore knee-length leather boots and a short skirt. I remember thinking: *why doesn't Helen wear anything like that?*

Two cocktails later and we were talking freely and laughing together. She talked about the clubs she liked to go to and the boyfriends she'd had. She was married, but never wore her ring. "I hate him. I want a divorce," she smiled as she sipped her drink.

I told her about Helen. "It feels like we're drifting apart. We don't talk about it, but I swear we both know it's happening. It feels like we never talk about anything important. Helen's not a warm, open person. Not like you."

"If you're not happy, you've got to get out. I've learned that much. You've got to think of yourself. Look after number one." Cassie fiddled with the green umbrella in her drink. "Sometimes a relationship is just too claustrophobic. I can't handle that. You have to act and feel in a certain way to appease your partner. It's a suppression of the self. It's all too complicated and I'm way too young to be fucked up by it." She laughed and knocked back the last of her drink.

"Yeah," I said, "it's been a long time since I've thought about myself."

The day before I fucked Cassie, I took Helen out driving on the estate. She felt confident enough to tackle the main roads. We drove down darkening avenues where terraced houses seemed to just collapse against each other. The roads got narrower the deeper we drove into the city.

She was doing well, until we reached the top of Old School Hill. A car came up behind us as Helen paused at the junction. She was struggling to find the Escort's breaking point. Her foot slipped on the clutch and the car began to roll backwards. The car behind reversed out of the way before Helen managed to crank the handbrake. Her face was flushed. She looked tired and miserable. "You all right?" I asked.

"Yes," she said, adjusting her feet on the pedals.

"The art of driving is control," I said. "You have to have complete control at all times."

"I know," she replied.

112

She hit the indicator and pulled out. She drove us home, parked outside of the flats. Then she broke down into tears.

"What's the matter?" I said, putting my arm around her.

"I just want to get it right," she said. "I want to get it perfect."

"It'll come," I said, stroking her face, "it'll come."

I fucked Cassie in her apartment during a Friday lunch hour. I don't know what I was expecting, but the whole thing felt mechanical and cold. I took her from behind and she whimpered and whispered dirty little words. I kept staring out of the window at the street below, at lines of faceless buildings and flecks of light from coffee shops and restaurants. After we'd dressed, I expected to feel cleansed, invigorated, but all I felt was a hollow emptiness. Cassie got shitty because I didn't talk. She combed her hair and reapplied her make-up in front of a tall ornate mirror, the same mirror she had been watching herself in moments before as we made love. We went back to work and we didn't speak a word to one another. At six o'clock I shuffled and stacked my papers and left the office.

Traffic was heavy; I was home after seven. The night built up like a wall against the window. The apartment was so silent and cold that I felt as if I'd walked into the wrong place. I paced the room. Our CDs lay scattered across the floor, and I thought I could discern a pattern in the way they were strewn. I stared at the Nigerian veneer we'd chosen from a South African-style furniture shop. It looked different now, irreparably changed. In fact the entire flat and its contents were different somehow. Little things – like our wind-chimes and DVDs and favourite books – no longer seemed so precious. I walked to the window and pulled back the curtain. The garden was dark. Streetlights and car lamps gleamed between thick dark trees and decrepit fencing. I let the curtain fall back in place and stared back at the flat. The silence felt endless and desperately empty.

Helen had tacked a note to the message board: *Popped to the 24-hour. See you soon.* I stared and stared at her writing until I began to cry.

"You're tired, you're tired," I whispered, and went to the

bathroom and showered.

I lay in bed staring at the ceiling. Helen slept soundlessly beside me. I was scared to touch her. Now and then I thought I could smell Cassie's perfume on my body so I sneaked out of bed and showered again. Eventually I slept, but I woke in the middle of the night from a nightmare. I'd been walking round and round in circles in the dark looking for Helen, but I couldn't find her.

Sitting up, I thought I saw Cassie grinning in the shadows. I blinked; saw it was just my coat hanging from the door.

Suddenly I realised Helen was gone. Kicking back sheets, I looked around. The door was open. Darkness spilled into the room.

I dressed and hurried to the window. Time seemed to pass in slow motion. The windowpane was dim and speckled with light that crawled out of the gaps between trees. Outside, Helen hurried past and vanished into the enveloping shadows. As I left the room, I heard the trees chuckle in the wind.

The moon had long gone; the sky was a whirlpool of shifting hues of black and purple: a puzzle trying to piece itself together. I pushed through twisted briars and nettles toward the churchyard. Tombstones leaned at peculiar angles. Helen stood beneath the drooping limbs of a dead willow tree, her fingers touching the marble angel behind the busy main road.

"Helen!" My voice trembled. She didn't hear me. The trees thrashed in the passing light of cars and lorries. I put my arm around her. She looked so cold and white that I thought she'd shatter, like glass. Then rain was everywhere, sharp in my eyes. I thought I was going to choke when Helen began screaming. There was blood all over the statue.

"Let's go," I said, holding her tight. As I dragged her away, glass scrunched beneath our feet.

"I can't breathe," whispered Helen once we were back inside our apartment. I lay her on the bed and checked her body for cuts. There were none. She kept wheezing and crying. "Why can't I breathe?" she repeated, over and over until she was asleep.

I paced the room. Stared out of the window and listened

to the razor-sharp wind rattling tall, dead trees. I returned to bed and closed my eyes.

I went searching for Helen in my dreams.

The morning was bathed in the soft cherry light of the early sun. At first, I had no real sense of the room around me. The warm hues raised my deteriorating spirits. I made breakfast and tidied the apartment as Helen showered. But an hour later the sky had clouded over. The walls faded in colour. I sat down in the corner and rubbed my eyes. When I was able to focus properly again, the walls seemed closer. I gazed out of the window.

Movement caught my eye. In the tangle of overgrowth beyond the clapboard fencing of our garden, a small family walked along the periphery of the churchyard. I stood and pressed my face close to the window and watched them pass. The young mother and father ushered their two small children around some purple, scraggly nettles. The little boy kept staring at the angel memorial sculpture jutting out of the long grass, encircled by weather-scarred tombstones. Then the pane was flecked with beads of rain. The young father took the hand of the little girl as he looked up at me. The young mother looked too.

Their eyes were like holes drilled in a glacier.

They stared straight through me, as if I wasn't there. I pushed my hands against the window and made myself as wide and as tall as I could, but I could still feel their eyes on the walls behind and around me. Then the family disappeared behind the trees. I wanted to shout, to scream. Then the rain was everywhere, formulating meaningless patterns on the windowpane.

Helen came into the room and wrapped her arms around me. I held her tight. She was crying; I could feel her tears against my face.

"I need to get out," I said. "I need fresh air."

She nodded and sat down on the bed. Running a hand through her hair, she stared at all her exotic pictures on the wall. "What's happening to us?" she said. "Why can't I connect with anything? The world seems to be drifting away from me."

I didn't know what to say to that. I buttoned up my coat. "Nothing can tear us apart. I've always said we're different, haven't I? We're different from others. We're not meant for this world. But we have each other, and that's enough to keep us going." I realised I was crying. "See you later," I whispered, and then took the flight of stairs down to the first floor where I pushed open the double doors and stepped outside. The rain came in great gusting sheets.

I kicked through the creepers and nettles to the churchyard. The sky was like glass; I imagined looking up and seeing the whole of the city reflected back at me. The angel stood in the long grass, her hands pressed together in front of her. She was grey but streaked with blue chips; it looked like she had a delicate network of veins. I stared into those serene black eyes. There was no blood streaked over her marble body, but then this didn't surprise me. A wreath of flowers fluttered in the wind barely a metre from the statue. There were more flowers piled close to the shadows of broken pines and rotting clapboard fencing.

"Perhaps I can go driving again tonight," said Helen as I prepared dinner that evening. She was looking brighter. She'd tied her hair into a ponytail and bought herself a new blouse in the shop round the corner. "What do you think?"

I smiled as I opened the oven and checked the lasagne. "Sure."

"Great."

Helen knelt by the CD player and rummaged through our record collection. The dreamy sound of *Spacemen 3* oozed through the speakers. I stood in the doorway to the kitchen, arms folded, watching her. "Love you," I said.

She turned and smiled at me, then went back to her CDs.

As Helen drove through the narrow lanes of the city, I was finding it increasingly hard to keep my eyes open. I don't know why I was feeling so tired. Perhaps my body had had enough of the real world and it wanted to shut down for a while. Helen's eyes speared straight ahead. Light from passing traffic washed across her face.

I kept falling in and out of sleep. When I opened my eyes, I caught flecks of streetlight and neon radiating from massage parlours, video rental shops and twenty-four hour cafes. Through the dark and rain I saw the lurid red neon dripping from the entrance to The Tap Room.

"I'd better drive us home," Helen said. She ran a hand through her hair.

We stopped at traffic lights. The rain rushed against the windscreen. The wipers screamed in their desperate battle against the deluge. I was aware of Helen tutting, resting her head against the window. Next thing I knew we were home. The car drew alongside the kerb. "Home," she sighed, cranking the handbrake. The motor was cut. There was just the rain.

When we got back into our apartment, I couldn't sleep. I lay there, staring at the ceiling. For a while, Helen was awake too. She nestled into me, her hand stroking my hair.

"I don't remember the drive," she whispered. "That's so disturbing. Isn't it?"

I kissed her face.

Then she was asleep, and I was wide awake.

I got up and walked to the window. It had stopped raining. I thought I saw people moving close to the road, close to the periphery of the churchyard, under the spectral glow of the streetlamps. I decided to take a walk outside, just to clear my head.

It was like walking in some other world. The trees were dark and washed with rain. Slate tombstones sliced out of the darkness. Nothing moved. I couldn't imagine anybody ever walking here.

The car was crumpled and broken, surrounded by broken fencing and tree limbs torn from their sockets. It had veered out of the road. In the shadows the angel sculpture glistened with thick, dark blood. Glass sparkled in the darkness like teeth. I saw the registration. It was our Escort. Helen's head hung from the shattered window, her neck half severed by the broken glass. I was there somewhere, head thrown back, a mush of splintered bone and clotted gore. There was blood all over the windscreen. Somewhere I could hear a siren wailing.

People were gathering, rustling and waving like thin trees in a storm. I walked away and returned to the flat, my hands fumbling through my pockets for the key.

It had begun to rain again. It pattered lightly against the window. I slipped into bed. Helen was fast asleep, her arm flung across her pillow.

I stared at the ceiling for a while, then rolled over and hugged Helen close and whispered in her ear that I loved her.

THE FIELDS

"Are you going to see Keira?" mother asked as soon as I was home.

I was lying on the sofa in the lounge, watching daytime TV. It was late June, but the weather was awful; outside, rain beat a steady tattoo against the front room window. "I don't know," I replied, shrugging.

"Why don't you know?"

"Because…things'll be *different* now."

"Only if you let them be different," she replied.

She got up from the rocking chair, stepped into the kitchen and started on the washing up. As I glanced at her, through the doorway, she said, "Keira's a lovely girl."

I sighed, rose and joined her, gathering up a tea towel from off the side. We stood there, shoulder to shoulder, Mum washing, me drying, as the rain streamed steadily down the kitchen window.

She said: "You're definitely going then."

"Yes, mum."

"For how long?"

"Think I've saved up enough for a year. Maybe two."

She nodded her head slowly, as if she hadn't heard me, and stared out of the window at the dark, dark fields.

I rang Keira after dinner.

It was weird hearing her voice again, after all this time. She sounded hesitant and vaguely distant, but I guess I should have expected that. I suggested meeting up in the Sun Inn, on the outskirts of Keighton, and to my relief she agreed.

It was a half hour walk to the pub, and despite my

119

reservations about meeting up with Keira again it was a comfort being out the house; mother's neediness had triggered the usual twinges of guilt.

Keira was there waiting for me when I arrived, sitting in an alcove at the back, nursing a glass of dry white wine.

"You're back, then," she said.

"Yeah," I smiled. "I'm back."

She raised an eyebrow. "Your Mum says you're not staying, though."

I pulled up a stool, disappointed by the subtle changes I discerned in her. I know it had been two, maybe three years, but I hadn't expected the dark circles around her eyes, the lines in her face, the tinge of grey to her hair. "What happened at uni?" I asked, concerned.

She explained that the course she was studying in Exeter – Media Studies – was crap. That and the fact she had no money meant she dropped out half way through the second year. She came back home and worked in the local convenience store, and on her father's farm.

"What about you?" she asked, chipped black fingernails tapping against her glass. "What did you do after uni?"

"I hung around in Birmingham. Rented a house in Solihull with some friends. I worked in the city for about a year and a half and saved up some money. Now I've come back for the summer. Mainly to keep Mum company, though."

She nodded slowly. "You haven't missed much," she said. "I mean, after all this time, nothing much has changed here."

We thought about that for a moment.

Suddenly, she said, "I take it you heard about my Dad."

"No," I said. "What happened?"

"He left us. Just walked out one night and never came back."

"Jesus."

"To tell you the truth, Mum and I both saw it coming. He'd been depressed for some time."

I finished my pint quickly. "Do you want to hang out for the summer?"

"I don't know, Glen. Don't you think it'll be weird?"

"Only if you let it be weird," I replied.

Rain rapped the windows, crackled against the tin roof of the shed outside, sloshed through the broken guttering. I heard a deep-throated growl of thunder, and the shaded lamp in the hall flickered ominously.

"Did you hear that?" whispered mother, suddenly, looking up from her Catherine Cookson paperback.

"What?"

"That was a knock, wasn't it? At the door."

She got up from her seat. I turned and watched her pull the chain across the door, release the bolts, twist down the handle.

There, in the doorway, was our neighbour, Len Cley. He was shivering, his face painted with rain. "It's Jean," he whispered. "She's changed. They're all going, Rita."

I glanced back at the TV. "Ssh," said mother and I could feel her eyes on me.

"The farm ... the debts ... now this ... how am I supposed to go on? I'm next, Rita." He laughed nervously. "I *hear* them, see."

A clap of thunder muffled their voices. Then mother closed the door and sat back down in her rocking chair. She raked her hand through strands of greying hair, dragged it down the length of her face. A sudden flash of lightning sketched out the heavy lines all round her mouth and eyes.

"What was that all about?" I asked.

"Jean's gone."

"Where?"

Mother didn't reply. Instead, she leaned back in her chair and scrunched her eyes up real tight.

"I've bought a round the world ticket," I told Keira. "I'll be in Bali by October drinking beer on Kuta beach. Should be in Australia over Christmas. Tokyo by Easter. Imagine: the fish and coral waterscapes of the Great Barrier Reef; the neon-lit wonderland of Tokyo by night!"

"Sounds beautiful," smiled Keira, wistfully.

We sat down on the steps of the old Baptist church. It was

late afternoon, but the streets were deserted. Above us, the shape of the clouds formed a figure that loomed over the village with its bent, spindly arms half-raised.

"Why don't you come with me?" I asked, suddenly.

"There you go again!"

"What?"

"Talking as if we're sixteen, as if we're still going out together!"

She sighed. "I can't go anywhere. Not now. I have to stay here and look after Mum."

After a while, I said: "I remember when my Dad passed away. The sense of loss ... well, it's hard to put into words. But it must be worse for you. I mean, the not-knowing ... it must be horrible."

Keira laughed weakly. "We *know* where he's gone, Glen."

She stood then, smoothing her hair behind her ears. I followed her gaze to the weeds spouting from the pavement across the road, to the cow dung smeared into the gutter, the shattered windows of the derelict cottages opposite. Around us a dry, musty smell filled the air. It made me think of old barns, of hay and straw and slow decay.

"There's a lot of tired people in this village," she said. "They're sick; they've had enough." She turned to look at me. "And they don't care who they taint, Glen. Not anymore."

I heard the chair. Creaking. Creaking. I closed the door behind me.

"Glen? Is that you?"

"Yes Mum," I called, hanging my jacket up on the banister. "It's me."

She didn't look around as I entered the living room, and I stood there a moment, in the doorway, watching her rock backwards and forwards in her chair.

"I had a dream," she said, softly. "Of how your life would be."

She laughed. "The fields are calling, Glen."

"The fields?"

She closed her eyes.

"Mum?"

I knelt down beside her.
She was asleep.

The telephone.
My eyes snapped open.
The telephone was ringing.
I dashed downstairs. The living room was empty. Mother's chair was still rocking, but now the front door was open – wide open. I glanced at the telephone. Snatched up the receiver.
"Glen?"
"Keira?"
"It's happening," she whispered. "It's my turn now. They want me. And I don't think I can fight it."
"Keira? Keira, listen to me..."
She hung up.
I dashed outside. The garden was deserted. Ahead, in the street, I caught a flash of white and realised it was mother.
I followed her around the back of some old stone cottages, out into the darkness of a field. She was clambering over a stile into the next field along so I ran, mud squelching and splashing beneath my feet.
The second field wasn't empty – there were figures everywhere. I stopped, breathless and afraid. I looked around.
"Mum?"
The figures swayed, their faces empty; dead. Keira was standing in the midst of them, silent and afraid. She turned to me and I grabbed hold of her arm. "Come on," I said. "Let's get out of here."
Hand in hand we pushed our way to the stile. At one point I thought I saw mother, standing in the darkness with her arms half-raised. But when I blinked, I saw that it wasn't her at all – just another one of those terrible figures.
I dragged Keira to the stile. The dead things rustled, brushing us with their hands. I clambered over, then held my arms out to her. But Keira had stopped, dead still, barely a metre away from me. She met my eyes. Blank. Empty. Her head sagged. There was straw in her mouth.
The night breathed. The dead things shuddered.

And from somewhere out in the field, mother called my name...

ALWAYS THE PAST

I resigned from my post as a recruitment officer in an employment agency, bored and disillusioned with the fast and useless pace of office life.

Instead, I spent time writing down by the brook, the park, or the cemetery. Locksley's a small but thriving town on the periphery of the city. The council are planning major renovations to boost commerce in the area – they want to drain the brook and bulldoze some woodland to make way for houses and construction sites. I devoted afternoons picketing with concerned members of the community, staging peaceful demonstrations near East Knell, but the businessmen and property developers will have the renovators in before the year is out.

My dole helps pay the rent on my apartment. I live above a dusty antique shop. The old man who owns it is friendly and quiet but is having extensive treatment for bone cancer, so he is in and out of hospital. I don't know what will happen to me once he dies. My back window overlooks the rear of Locksley Church and cemetery – it is quite eerie at night to look out of the window and see gravestones projecting out of the darkness.

It was in the churchyard that I saw Kieran for the first time.

He was wading through wild nettles and creepers, a camera hanging from a cord around his neck. I pressed close to the window, and the long, fine hairline crack in the glass distorted his body as he wove between slate tombstones. He appeared captivated by one particular stone angel, kneeling solemnly beneath the limbs of some long dead willow trees.

He'd touch her face, tracing his fingers over smooth, cold marble.

Kieran fascinated me for days. After sunset he'd be there, standing in the foliage, encircled by pale memorials and headstones.

Then, one evening, he caught me watching him.

My heart skipped a beat. He stared long and hard at me, then shrugged his shoulders and kicked his way through the creepers. I breathed easy again, shrunk from the window, watched him disappear behind the back of the old, dilapidated church.

That night I dreamed I was at a party in somebody's house. I thought I recognised the house at the time, but when I woke I knew I'd never been there before. Heavy rock crackled and spat from invisible speakers. I heard couples laughing as they danced and groped in the living room. When I looked up all I could see were their knotted and tangled shadows flickering across the walls.

I drifted toward the kitchen in search of alcohol, but somebody was standing in the doorway, blocking the way. He was short and strange-looking with pointed ears and the blackest eyes. I wondered whether those eyes reflected everything, or absolutely nothing at all. He was wearing thick red lipstick and mascara.

"I know you," he said.

"I don't think so," I replied, trying to squeeze past him, but his pale hand was on my shoulder.

"Yes, yes I do. We've met before."

"No."

My head swam with music and empty, dark shapes. I threw off his hand and slipped past him into the kitchen.

I found a bottle of vodka, unscrewed the top, breathed in its sharp fumes.

The strange-looking man placed a hand on my hip, his breath fetid and warm on my neck.

"You must remember me."

"Who are you?" I whispered.

"We know each other *inside out*."

His long, wet tongue was in my ear. I pushed him away

and he stood frozen against the wall, a monstrous grin all over his face.

I realised we were alone.

All the couples had gone.

"Hi," I said.

Kieran didn't seem particularly surprised to see me.

"Hi. Are you the person who lives over there? I thought I saw you in the window yesterday."

"Yes," I said, nodding. "Sorry, I didn't mean to be nosy."

He smiled. "That's okay. You don't mind me traipsing around here?"

"No. No, of course not. Why would I mind?"

"I don't know. Perhaps you've got somebody buried here, a relation, a friend perhaps."

"No."

"Some people don't take too kindly to others trampling across graveyards, taking photographs." He laughed. "I'm Kieran."

"Alice."

He extended a hand and I shook it, glancing into his fine, black glass eyes. I pushed a strand of hair behind my ear. Cold wind moaned through the cemetery, sweeping dead leaves between headstones.

"I guess it is kind of disrespectful."

"Disrespectful?" I was miles away.

"Walking over graves. Taking photographs. *Disturbing the dead.*" He spoke in a mock Bela Lugosi accent. We both laughed.

"So why do you?"

"I don't know, to tell you the truth." He edged toward the angel, raised his camera, took a quick picture. "I guess I'm fascinated by death. God, you must think I'm morbid. Well you're right, I suppose. I am."

"Are you a professional photographer?"

"No. I do this because I want to."

I nodded to the angel, my hair licking and whipping about my face. "She's beautiful."

Then Kieran said a very strange thing. I thought he was

127

joking, but a peculiar light in his eyes convinced me otherwise. "She's alive," he whispered. "I really believe she's alive."

Just as he took the photograph, and as the flash danced over her body, I noticed some stone flake away from the statue.

Kieran didn't have a job. He lived in a bedsit in Wickham, close to the multi-complex cinema and TGI Friday. He earned money busking in the shopping precinct. He played popular songs to shoppers with a beat-up acoustic guitar. Occasionally he modelled for sixth-form art students at Wickham College. He caught buses to different suburbs in the city, taking pictures of cemeteries and churches, sometimes of dead birds and road-kills decomposing in the asphalt of major roads.

I kind of latched onto him; there was nothing else to do. I scanned *The Locksley Chronicle* and read that the council was already pulling down trees on East Knell common. Everything that mattered was dissolving around me. I didn't even like my apartment; there was nothing between those damp, rotting walls except my own languishing impression.

My writing deteriorated. It was as if words no longer made sense to me. I read and re-read my poems and stories but found them meaningless, so I tore them to shreds. Kieran didn't mind me hanging around. I'd wait for him to appear in the cemetery, perched on a tomb, watching the sun melt behind those tall, black church spires.

One night I dreamed I was in this room that I vaguely recognised. I knew somebody else was in the room because I could hear breathing. I sat up and for a second saw the form of a man in the corner struggling to tear a plastic bag from off his face. He was thrashing his limbs but the bag just sucked in tighter and I knew he was suffocating. I wanted to do something, but couldn't move.

The strange-looking man stood over him, smiling darkly, eyes smudged with purple make-up, thin lips painted a lurid crimson.

"Do something," I said.

The strange-looking man laughed – a real horrible laugh, like the sound of a record when it's slowed down.

"You are mine," he said. "I made you, you belong to me. You always will belong to me."

One dreary morning Kieran and I met in a café.

We sat in the corner, under a print of *Café Terrace at Arles*. Like all of van Gogh's work, it burned with feverish, otherworldly life. When we weren't talking, the violent hiss of the rain filled the void.

"Why do you take all these weird pictures?" I asked.

Kieran stared at me, shrugged, then stirred his coffee with a plastic spoon. "Alice," he whispered, "some people can't face the darker things in life. They pretend bad things don't exist. They shut them out."

He discerned the puzzled look on my face.

"Come with me," he said.

He took me to his bedsit, a five-minute walk into Wickham. We cut across the old disused railway bridge and the deserted, rain-swept park. As he struggled with the key in the lock, I noticed a black cat watching me from underneath a gutted Escort.

Overhead, in the direction of the multi-complex cinema, came the low rumble of thunder. Rain made hypnotic circles in puddles. He pushed open the door, turned, and smiled at me.

"Come in. It's not much, but it's home."

The room was bare and dark, furnished only by a couple of chairs placed close to the sink. There was no television, no ornaments, no table; just a few esoteric-looking books piled up on a windowsill. I noticed apparatus for developing photographs in the corner. Photographs hung from pegs on a clothesline stretched out across the length of the flat, and I stopped and stared at them.

Shadowy, half-lit streets.

A man weeping by a mausoleum.

Small mounds of fresh earth in an overgrown back garden.

A handsome young man lying on a tomb, scribbling notes into a small black book.

I recognised the places, but Kieran had created a mood through lighting and detail to make them *different* somehow.

"They're brilliant," I whispered. "You *should* be professional."

"It's something I want to do for *me*. Nobody else."

"But that's such a waste," I said.

"It's the way I want it to be."

"Do you have a job? Friends? Family?"

"No. I've never worked. I'm not close to anybody really. I can't fit in, out there."

I pushed a strand of hair behind my ear. Perhaps I was being silly and immature; perhaps I was a sixteen-year old girl again, but it felt as if I had found my soul mate, someone who thought and felt exactly like me.

"I like to be on the outside of things," he said. "To live *around* what we see and know. It's not that I don't want to connect with society; it's just that I can't. I can't do it."

I drifted to the furthest corner of the room where there were dozens and dozens of photographs of Locksley Cemetery. The otherworldly lighting made me think of spirit planes and places I had only walked in dreams.

Kieran opened a bottle of wine. "Why are you so intrigued by me?" he asked.

I stared at the uncarpeted floor. "You're interesting, I guess. Different. I think I'd like to know you better."

"I'm not interesting." He took two glasses from off the sideboard. "There's nothing profound about me." He laughed to himself, then leaned back against the wall. "People need anchors in life. Just to keep them sane. People need truth and certainty to give their lives happiness...and stability. I can't offer any of those things. I can't believe in anything that I see around me so I kind of create my own worlds."

I wondered what had made him this way.

"Why are you so fascinated by death?" I looked back at his photographs. "Is this a way of confronting your demons?"

He looked uncomfortable. He stared at his hands and I felt embarrassed, frightened that I'd grieved him with my question.

"I don't know," he said with a slow shrug of his shoulders. "I'm scared, Alice. Doors have been opened...gateways. And there are things coming through that..." He stopped suddenly, blinked, laughed humourlessly. "What frightens *you*, Alice?"

I shrugged. "The Spook."

He narrowed his eyes. "Who?"

"He's this strange-looking guy who appears in my dreams. I call him The Spook. I think he knows everything about me."

"Everything?"

"It's like he can open up my soul just by looking at me."

We fell silent; there was just the rain.

After we'd finished his bottle of wine, we made love in his bed.

That night I wandered a street that I almost recognised. From above, the moon cast a pale, greasy smear on to the pavement.

I ascended an iron-cast staircase, disappeared into the shadows of a building that smelt of long lost days and dead things. There was a mirror on a wall and I caught sight of my own petrified reflection floating in darkness. From somewhere far off I heard horrible, echoey laughter.

Somebody flicked a switch and lurid crimson lighting flooded the room. I noticed somebody bound to a chair with a plastic bag over his head. Gnarled tree limbs scratched at a windowpane, but I couldn't remember there being trees outside. The laughter grew louder, and I heard metal scraping against the dried-up old bones of the building.

I woke suddenly to find Kieran gone. I dressed and watched the rain sweep across the common. It felt like I'd been alone all along. The thought of returning to my apartment overwhelmed me with dread.

Kieran had left a note tacked to the door: *Alice, see you soon. Kieran.*

We were reunited that evening in the cemetery.

He stood gazing at the angel under the willows. I leaned against some railings, hands shoved into the pockets of my jeans, listening to the trees creak and sigh around me. He took several pictures, hung his camera around his neck, then drifted off behind the church.

I drew back a curtain of sharp branches and gazed into her eyes.

Her face seemed different somehow; the lines of her features less defined. I pressed my hand to her face.

Slowly, very softly, some more stone flaked away beneath

my fingertips.

"Kieran, when will I see you again?" I asked. He paused at the cemetery gates. He looked tired and pale, and nettles and twigs clung to his coat and hair. "Can I come back with you?"

"Sorry, Alice," he replied. "I want to be alone this evening. I'm not in the mood for company tonight."

"Oh. Okay." I felt crushed. "You'll be back here tomorrow, won't you?"

"Perhaps."

It began to drizzle so I wrapped my cardigan around me.

"I like you, Alice. You remind me of somebody I once knew. You're a special person and I like you very much." Rain came down harder, tearing through the trees. "It's that...it's harder for me to get close to people these days. I find it hard to give pieces of myself away."

"It's okay. We can take our time." My voice trembled. He stooped and kissed me, running a hand through my hair. Then he was gone, into the rain.

I perched on my bed, staring at the walls. Gradually, the shadows lengthened across the ceiling and floor. I began to see things in the half-light, transient images of shapes and faces distorted like fleeting reflections in a broken mirror.

I laid my head down on the pillow.

The night's sky reflected back the lurid light of the city, masking the moon and stars. I saw no signs of life in the buildings around me, heard no traffic, no voices. I looked around, and noticed a phone box on the corner of the street. I had to call Kieran, to warn him about the danger he was in, so I opened the door and squeezed myself into the cubicle. The light above my head flickered on and off, and every time I gazed at the smooth black glass of the booth I saw my pale, translucent reflection disappear then reappear, disappear then reappear.

I picked up the receiver.

"Kieran?"

No answer. Just an empty, mind-numbing hiss. Then the voice.

"I'll be here for you, Alice."

"Who?"

"Stop playing games."

That slowed-down laugh.

Then, a flash of disjointed images:

A door opening.

Darkness spilling into a room.

Kieran trying to free his hands and the polythene bag over his head.

A painted grin.

The glint of a knife.

"Have you ever felt slighted, Alice? Do you think sometimes that you're just walking one long, dark corridor for the whole of eternity?"

"Where are you?"

"I'm with you now, Alice."

I slammed the phone down. I ran a shaky hand through my hair. Then I saw the Spook standing outside the booth, and I screamed. His monstrous face glared in at me, dark eyes wide and crazed, spittle dribbling down from black, scabbed lips.

I woke.

Night poured through the window.

I crossed the room, snapping on all the lights, half expecting *him* to be waiting.

When I looked into the mirror minutes from dawn, I saw a laceration across my neck. I touched it with trembling fingers and it opened like a wide red mouth.

I waited patiently at the window for Kieran to show. The afternoon dragged into evening, but he never appeared.

By eight o'clock, the sunset had transformed gnarled trees and shuttered houses into silhouettes. I drifted down the narrow staircase, listening to the cough of the old man in the dusty antique shop. I scrambled over clapboard fencing, kicked my way through nettles and thick, ugly creepers. I saw The Spook standing under the shadow of the church, watching me intently, rubbing his pale hands together. When I looked again, he metamorphosed into a stone gargoyle right in front of my eyes, black lips curling into an eternal and abhorrent sneer. I shivered and pressed on.

I searched the cemetery, stooping to look behind and between tombstones. I couldn't find him.

Eventually I stumbled upon the angel, brooding under those old willows, looking so sad and frail.

Then, as I turned right the way around, I caught sight of a memorial sculpture I had never seen before staring at me from tall yellow grass.

Recognition clicked as I met hollow black eyes.

I stepped back and felt cold stone against my hands and realised he wasn't looking at me at all.

I returned to my apartment, dug through some cardboard boxes under my bed, and found a Polaroid camera amongst my old clothes and books.

I crossed the cemetery. The moon was full and stars were scattered like chips of glass. Behind rust-eaten railings, willow trees hung thick and silent. Brushing away dirt and twigs with the back of my hand, I knelt before my angel. And as I raised the camera with trembling fingers, I wondered if my pictures could ever be half as good as one of Kieran's.

DEAD AND BURIED

Just off the freeway, a hundred miles from Cyclona Springs, Peggy cut the lights of her Citroen. The moon watched on, pale and scratched in a star-washed sky.

She cried then; great wracking sobs shook her body. In the blackness of the windscreen, her dead white reflection jerked, swayed and shuddered.

She woke, sometime later, with a start.

Everything was silent. The desert rippled like an alien ocean: all blue and purple hues. Opening the door, she stepped outside and shivered.

Half a mile from the car she came across the first face, staring up at her with dead black eyes. Around her, glowing brightly, shone more white casts – arms, hands, faces, slicing eerily out of the dunes.

Nothing in Peggy's life felt real anymore. Her world had collapsed, she felt dead inside.

She'd left work early yesterday afternoon, having complained of a migraine. She got home around three, saw the red Fiesta in the drive, a car she hadn't recognised.

As she let herself in, she saw them on the sofa together: James, with his arms wrapped around the waist of a blonde she hadn't seen before, the girl jerking up and down in his lap.

Peggy rubbed her eyes, tried to rub the image clean away. The wedding ring on her finger looked cheap, ugly to her now. She fixed her eyes ahead. The freeway unspoiled, long, dark, lonely.

Peggy glanced anxiously at the fuel gauge – the Citroen was

almost out of gas.

The rain came suddenly, unexpectedly, the desert's first downpour in over a year. Through its dirty veil she saw the gas station ahead, and dropped her shoulders with relief.

Pulling up, she killed the engine as the rain beat a steady tattoo against some discarded oil drums in the yard. Every time she glanced up at the windscreen she saw her own dead white reflection.

A tap on the window jolted her from her thoughts, and she quickly wound the window down. A man dressed in oil-smeared dungarees and a baseball cap stuck his face into the car. "Want me to fill her up?"

"Yes," Peggy, nodded. "Yes, that would be fine. Thank you."

He nodded his head slowly. "You can run on in if you like," he said, waving a hand toward the office. "My wife'll fix up the bill."

Closing the door behind her, Peggy cuffed the rain from her eyes.

The office was dark, the blinds down.

"You poor thing!" came a voice, and Peggy turned quickly. Standing behind the counter was a woman in a faded floral dress and jeans. "Look at you, soaked through to the bone! Wait, let me fetch you a towel."

Peggy moved to the nearest window, peered through a blind. "Your poor husband," she said. "He's going to drown out there."

"Oh, don't worry about Stan; he's big and ugly enough to look after himself!"

Peggy took a towel from the woman and patted her hair with it. "Don't you get a bit lonely living out here?"

The woman shrugged. "No, not really. We like it out here. You see, it's what God wants us to do, to help…" Her voice trailed off.

Stan burst into the office, sopping wet. "Darn filthy weather," he muttered, wiping his eyes. "Ain't no sign of it ceasing, either."

"How much do I owe you?" Peggy asked.

"Twenty-one dollars, miss."

The woman moved behind the counter, rang it up on the till. As Peggy handed over the money, their hands brushed and a strange, troubled look crossed the woman's face. Embarrassed, Peggy turned away.

"Wait," the woman said, reaching for her. "You don't want to be driving in this weather. Come downstairs with me and we'll talk some more. Not often we get to talk to people, ain't that right, Stan?"

Stan moped his face with a handkerchief. "Damn right, Chrissie. Pretty quiet out here, most of the time."

"Thanks, but I really must be going."

Chrissie lifted the counter. There was something strange about her eyes – they seemed to *glow* in the darkness. Quickly Peggy made a move for the door, but Stan slapped a hand on her shoulder. "Now why don't you go along with Chrissie there, little lady."

The woman took Peggy's arm. "Yes, come with me. I know how *lonely* you're feeling. It's horrible when your world feels so dead."

What does she mean? Peggy thought, alarmed. *She can't possibly know...*

"I'll leave you two to it," sniffed Stan, tugging his baseball cap down over his head. "Better get the old pickup fixed 'fore tomorrow..."

Chrissie led Peggy through a door behind the counter to a stairwell which spiralled down into a kind of basement room. "After you," Chrissie said, extending a hand, eyes shining.

Peggy thought of pushing the woman down the stairs, of running for the car, but Stan was standing in front of the office door, blocking her exit.

Slowly, tentatively, she placed one foot in front of the other, edging down into a dark, musty, subterranean room.

She thought: *This isn't happening. In a minute you're going to wake from this nightmare.*

The room was lit by candles fluttering from tall, ornate stands. In the centre of the stone floor was a battered sofa and an easy chair, sitting quiet on top of a straw mat, patterned with hook-shaped moons and cherub-faced suns. And pinned to a board on the far wall were dozens and dozens of photographs.

The room was cold. You couldn't hear the rain down here.

"Why are there candles?" Peggy whispered.

"No electricity down here, my love."

Peggy walked toward the photographs on the wall. Faces smiled back at her, each one naggingly familiar. A man with a neat goatee beard, smartly dressed in a pinstriped suit. A woman with black hair and pretty green eyes. A teenage boy with red-rimmed spectacles and dishevelled dark locks. A balding, middle-aged man with sharp pale-grey eyes and sallow face.

The desert.

Oh Jesus, the faces from the desert.

"They were sad," sighed Chrissie, nodding her head at the photos. "But then they found me."

Peggy touched the walls. They were solid. Soundproof.

"I want to go," Peggy said. "*Now.*"

Chrissie took a step toward her, her eyes pure white now. Blind.

"Lie down," she instructed.

Peggy let out a strangled cry, staggered backwards, fell into the sofa. "Don't hurt me," she whispered.

Standing over her, Chrissie reached up with her fingers and pierced the flesh under her chin with her nails. Then she peeled her face clean off, like a mask. There was no bone, no blood underneath, just a flash, an intense, searing whiteness that blinded Peggy and cut short the scream in her throat.

Then nothing.

Peggy breathed in warm morning air.

It was going to be a hot one. The sun was rising over the freeway, scorching the asphalt.

"Smile, dear."

Peggy turned just as Chrissie snapped a picture of her with an old Polaroid camera.

The woman waited a moment for the picture to develop,

then held the photograph up to the light. "Something to remember you by."

Stan started the engine to the pickup. As Peggy glanced toward it, she noticed a ghost-white hand had slipped out from beneath a sheet of yellowing canvas in the back...saw the wedding ring on one of its fingers. "Better make that trip to the desert," he sighed, leaning out the driver's window and tipping his cap. "Nice to have met you, miss."

"You too." Peggy nodded, smiling.

Chrissie was beside her then. "Remember," she whispered, "there are worlds and worlds inside of you."

Then, as the pickup pulled away, throwing clouds of smoke into the air, Chrissie was gone, leaving Peggy alone with the freeway, but no longer afraid.

STORY NOTES

These 19 stories were written over a space of 13 years, from 1995 to 2008. Most of these stories have been previously published; a few of them are published here for the first time. Nearly all the published stories have been revised for this collection.

Now That I've Lost You

This was previously published in 2003 in *Wicked Hollow #5*. *Wicked Hollow* was a very cool, pocket-sized mag; because of its size, I was able to sneak it into work to read on the sly! I always liked the title of this story, and felt it summed up this collection nicely.

Dead City Blues

It took me quite a while to knock this one into shape. A friend suggested changing the tense from past to present, giving it a greater sense of urgency and pace, and it seems to have worked. This one was previously unpublished, and yes I have watched most of those movies on Steven's shelf...

Mine

Another unpublished piece. I wrote this for editor and writer Jodi Lee's anthology *Courting Morpheus* and although it made the shortlist, it didn't quite make the final cut. The anthology was about a fictional town called New Bedlam, and it centred on the horrors released by that town's own insomniac resident authors. Jodi very kindly allowed me to use the name New Bedlam for this collection.

Eleanora
This was published way back in 2002 in Graeme Hurry's excellent *Kimota*.

Death's Door
This was published in a slightly different form as 'Step Over' in *Not One of Us*. However, I was never really happy with that story, particularly the ending, so I had a go at rewriting it and this was the result. It was published as 'Death's Door' on the *Whispers of Wickedness* website in 2005.

One of Their Own
Published in *Black Petals #39*. While revising it for this collection, I had the idea to use recurring motifs and characters to give the collection a sense of 'wholeness'.

A Place the Night Can't Touch
One of my early pieces, I was delighted to see this published in *Darkness Rising #6: Evil Smiles,* edited by Len Maynard and Mick Simms. I was a big fan of their Enigmatic Tales and Darkness Rising anthologies, and after a few rejections finally managed to slip this one past them. Incidentally, my brother and students at the Surrey Institute of Art and Design made a short film based on this one. It's really good (a vast improvement on the story, I think!).

Highways
Previously published in Trevor Denyer's influential *Midnight Street* magazine, 'Highways' earned me my first honourable mention in Ellen Datlow's The Year's Best Fantasy and Horror. It had been known as 'The Tear', but I much preferred Trevor's idea for a title.

The Dispossessed
This short-short found a home in the first issue of *Cemetery Moon* in 2008, a US magazine edited by Chris Pisano.

STORY NOTES

Painting Blind Circles
This earned me my second honourable mention in the Year's Best Fantasy and Horror. It was published in an anthology called *Dark Doorways,* edited by James Cooper, in 2006.

Cure
My second ever published story. Dave Price, editor of *Tales of the Grotesque and Arabesque,* did a great job in knocking my clumsy prose into shape, and I was delighted to see it in print in ToGA way back in 1999. It was called 'Alone' then; when I revised it in 2005 for *Whispers of Wickedness* I changed the title to 'Cure'. I remember someone writing on the Whispers of Wickedness message board that the tourist board in Goa wouldn't be thanking me for this one!

Anja
A previously unpublished story, written specially for this collection.

Loretta
I'm hardly what you call prolific, and it's painful the amount of time I can spend on a single sentence let alone a whole short story, but 2005 was quite a productive year for me. I managed to see 6 (yes, a whole six!!) stories published that year including this one, in *Dark Fire* E-Zine.

The Night Is Mine
This was an unpublished piece that had been sitting around in a drawer for a while. Finally managed to get it into a reasonable shape for this collection. Used to be called 'Dead Ends'.

All We Have
Published in *Black Petals #42.* Dark, short and weird. Bit like me, really!

The Art of Driving
Previously published in *The Dream Zone #4* in 1999, *The Best*

of The Dream Zone, and more recently in the anthology *Sleep Walkin' & Pick Lockin'*. I came up with the idea while working in some heinous call centre in Hampshire, and it shares its title with a song by Black Box Recorder.

The Fields
Written in 2005, I found a home for 'The Fields' in the first issue of *Theatre of Decay,* a print magazine from the US. I'd always wanted to write a creepy story involving scarecrows (scarecrows rock!) and here's the result.

Always the Past
Another very early story, published in *Kimota #13* in 2000. The Spook was very much inspired by David Lynch's Mystery Man from *Lost Highway*, an all-time favourite film of mine.

Dead and Buried
I'm extremely fortunate to have been published in so many wonderful small press zines. I look back on the 'golden age' of the small press with a great deal of fondness and affection. Mad to think there were people out there putting these mags together with so little time and money, but still doing a great service to writers and illustrators alike. Here's another quality zine: *The Edge: Tales of Suspense.* 'Dead and Buried' appeared in issue 18, and it felt a fitting end to this collection.

Paul Edwards
April 2011

ABOUT THE AUTHOR

Paul Edwards was born and raised in Bristol, but now lives in the Somerset market town of Frome. To date he's had over 40 publications in a wide range of magazines, anthologies and webzines, and has had 2 honourable mentions in the *Year's Best Fantasy and Horror*. One of his stories, 'A Place the Night Can't Touch', was made into a short film by students at The Surrey Institute of Art and Design. His debut collection *Black Mirrors* was published by Rainfall in May 2012 and he's currently hard at work on a novel and a third collection. When he's not writing, he enjoys drinking local cider, spending time with his family and watching horror movies late into the night...

Praise for Paul Edwards and *Black Mirrors*:

"Vibrant story-telling with delicious twists and turns...I'm happy to declare Paul Edwards is a new talent to watch."
— Simon Clark, author of *The Night of the Triffids*.

"Paul Edwards is an exciting new talent on the horror scene. With this collection he's already proving he has every attribute needed to develop into a highly successful author."
— John B. Ford, author of *The Evil Entwines*.

3049757R00076

Printed in Great Britain
by Amazon.co.uk, Ltd.,
Marston Gate.